All The Dope Boys 'Gon Feel Her 2

JAHQUEL J.

To join my mailing list, be sure to visit my website:
www.jahquel.com
Be sure to join my reader's group. They receive all updates and
announcements first.
Jahquel J's "We Reading or Nah?" Group
Find me on social media:
Facebook: Jahquel J.
Instagram: @Jahquel_
TikTok: @IamJah

$\mathcal{S}ynopsis$

In book one, Kenni's path leads her to Virginia, where she unexpectedly runs into Haze. After years without seeing him, she quickly realizes that time has been good to him. He is no longer the next-door neighbor with busted shoes and hand-me-down clothes. Now he has the money, cars, and jewelry that once caught Kenni's attention, the very things he did not have back then. As Kenni struggles through her ongoing issues with Bridge, Haze becomes a welcome distraction from her reality. There is just one problem. Haze is in a serious relationship with his girlfriend, Whitney.

When Hans moved away with his brother, he never imagined he would cross paths with Saylor again. Fate, however, had other plans and placed her back in his life. Back home, Saylor had always been the one who caught his attention. He loved everything about her, and for a brief moment they shared a small fling. Now older and more experienced, Hans is ready to leave his player ways behind and make Saylor his woman.

The problem is Saylor is tangled in a complicated triangle with Darren and Brix. While Saylor believes she is simply being a supportive friend to Darren, he sees their connection as something more. After running into Brix, old feelings resurface, and they find themselves dancing around emotions they never fully resolved. Saylor is still hurt that Brix chose Juleena, and Brix is still wounded that Saylor did not fight harder for their relationship.

In this finale, Kenni and Saylor search for what true love truly feels like. Their journeys are filled with twists and turns, but when love is real, it finds a way. Will Kenni find the courage to walk away from Bridge? Will Saylor choose to reignite a love from her past? Find out in part two of All The Dope Boys Gon' Feel Her.

Juleena sat across the street from the diner she followed Brix to. She had watched him order food, take a few calls, and eat his food. She knew it looked foolish to follow her man, and she wished that she had more confidence in him to trust his word. Except, Brix told her he was going to grab some food in the hood, not Richmond, Virginia. Today was her son's recital and she had a limited time to make it back to Maryland in time, but something wouldn't allow her to pull off. She needed to know why he had lied to her. The cellphone ringing in her cup holder caused her to jump out of her skin. Grabbing it, she pressed the green icon button on the screen and put the phone to her ear.

"Mama, what do you need?"

"Where are you? The recital is in an hour and the boys are asking where you are." Juleena looked at her watch and knew she wouldn't make it back in time.

"Mama, cover for me. I'm busy at the shop and can't get away," she lied.

"Which one? I can drive them by so they can see you before we head to the school."

"This nigga," Juleena blurted when she saw Saylor walking into the diner. They both hugged and then Saylor sat down across from him.

"What nigga?" Jessica asked. "What are you talking about Juleena?"

"I'm sitting here watching Brix with another woman," Juleena's voice cracked.

Jessica sighed. She loved Brix like a son, but knew he wasn't in love with her daughter. She could see that he settled. He may have loved her daughter, but he wasn't in love with Juleena. Jessica had tried to tell Juleena a while ago and she refused to hear it. Brix never wanted the kids, picket fence, and relationship that Juleena craved.

"Baby, I told you about Brix long ago. That man isn't feeling what you're feeling."

"Mama, I don't want to hear this shit right now. Brix loves me, he chose me."

Jessica ended the call because she knew there was no getting through to Juleena. She had warned her a long time ago that their relationship was one sided. Jessica loved Brix because although he didn't feel the same way Juleena did, he cared for her grandson and treated Juleena with respect.

"I can't believe this," Juleena said to herself. She wanted to get out the car and beat Saylor down. Instead, she turned her car on and pulled away from the diner.

With tears pouring down her eyes, she searched her GPS for the directions to make it back home. She was so consumed with the GPS that she didn't notice that she sped through a red light. Juleena didn't notice until a truck plowed into the driver's side of her car. Her head knocked against the window and she fell unconscious.

* * *

What was supposed to be a weekend had turned into a week. Kenni enjoyed every little bit of time she spent with Meeka. She drove over to Meeka's house to chill with her. Kenni never understood why she and Saylor never hung out with Meeka instead of India. Meeka was down to earth, chill, and about her family. The way she loved on her daughter and baby's father was admirable. Her baby's father, Kook, was a little touched in the head, but Kenni could see how much he loved her.

"You want a wine cooler? We can sit outside on the porch and chat," Meeka asked.

"Peach please," Kenni told her and they went onto the porch to sit.

Kook and Meeka's daughter, Aero, was asleep inside. Meeka crossed her legs and looked at Kenni, who was enjoying the breeze and her wine cooler.

"Be honest with me, Ken."

"About?"

"You and Bridge. Girl, you came for a weekend and haven't left. What's up with you and him?"

Kenni felt like she could trust Meeka. They spent all week together and Meeka had been nothing but real with her. She welcomed her into her home, she met her man and daughter. She sighed. "Bridge fucks all types of bitches behind my back, in my face and doesn't make any apologies for it. He had three babies on me and made me loose about three babies. I'm just so sick and tired of the shit with him."

Meeka wasn't surprised. Before Kenni had gotten with Bridge, she heard he used to knock Mercedes around. His hand issues weren't anything new to her. She had heard and seen it all.

"I'm so sorry, Kenni." She rubbed her shoulder. "Why don't you just leave?"

"Because Bridge is all I've ever known. My mama left and he's the only one that has stood by my side. Every time I have the courage to leave, it goes away when I think about where I'm going to go."

Meeka hated that she was in this situation. "Shit, you can come stay here or with Saylor. You have places to go, you're just not ready to leave, babe."

"Why do I love a man that shows me over and over that he doesn't respect nor love me? I hate that I even love him as much as I do," she sighed.

"Your love is real, so that's why it's so hard for you to turn it off. Still, just because you love him doesn't mean you have to stay and put up with what he puts you through. A nigga doesn't have to put you through hell for you to feel like he loves you. He can simply just love you."

Kenni heard everything that Meeka said. She agreed with her for the most part about everything. Since she had been eighteen, she had looked at Bridge for everything. He was the one who upgraded her lifestyle. She was a hot girl living in Marcy projects, and he moved her to the finest condos and mansions. She drove the most exclusive cars and wore expensive designers. He was the one who enrolled her into college, and the same one who made her drop out. Everything in her life revolved around Bridge. She didn't see a future without him being near her. As stupid as it sounded, Bridge was her comfort zone. The abuse, lies, and cheating were just the price she paid for the lifestyle she had become accustomed to.

"Who that?" Kenni switched the subject. A black on black Bentley with dark tints pulled in front of Meeka's house.

"Oh, that's Kook's half-brother," she waved it off and took

a sip from her wine cooler. Kenni nodded and leaned back to sip her wine cooler. A caramel skinned woman stepped out of the car first. "Hey, Whitney!" Meeka called out and waved to the woman.

"Hey boo!" the girl yelled back.

Kenni watched as the girl switched over to the porch. The driver's side opened and a man hopped out with his back turned. When he came around the car, Kenni observed the tattoos that littered his arms and neck. His hair was pulled back into a ponytail. When she looked into his face, her mouth dropped.

"Haze?" she yelled out.

One

Kenni

I STOOD there as if time stopped and stared at Haze. He stared back at me and I took off running off the porch. It had been years since I've seen or heard about him. We all thought he was dead. Last me and Saylor heard was that Hans had got shot and both of them went off the radar. I reached out a few times and never heard anything back from him. Naturally, life continued and I went on about my life. Seeing him standing in front of me looking so grown up and fine, I ran and jumped into his arms. My arms never wanted to let go of his body. He held onto my body too, and the woman beside us sucked her teeth and cleared her throat a few times before he gently placed me back on the ground.

"How? Why? Where?" was all the words that came out of my mouth. It was hard trying to form a complete sentence because I didn't know what to make of all of this. Never would

I have imagined that I would run into Haze while visiting Meeka in Virginia.

Haze chuckled and hugged me once more before he spoke. "Damn, Kenni... You didn't age none." He smiled and looked me over good.

"Um, babe." The woman beside him snapped to get his attention. He turned to look at her, then looked at me again. "Haze!" she raised her voice.

"Whitney, chill for a second." He held his hand up and continued to pay me attention. "What you doing out here? I know you didn't leave New York." He still had my hand in his and rubbed his thumb over my hand. His touch brought chills to my body.

"I'm visiting Meeka for the week. I did move out of New York though," I blushed as I looked into his eyes. His braids were neatly braided to the back, and his clothes were the latest thing out. It was a far cry from the bum clothes he wore on the regular when we were younger.

"Oh word? How long you out here?"

"I don't know yet." Bridge had been calling and begging me to come home and I had to admit, I was ready to toss everything into my car and head home. Seeing Haze made me want to stay in Virginia just a little bit.

"I came to drop Whitney off and talk to my brother real quick... I wanna get up with you. Yo, where Saylor? Ya'll still cool?"

I laughed. "Boy, you know Saylor is my sister. Even when we're not speaking, we're still good," It didn't matter what me and Saylor went through, we were more than friends. Saylor was my sister and nothing could break us apart.

"I wanna see her too..." he allowed his voice to trail off.

I stared at him and couldn't help but to lick my lips and

bite down on the corner of it. This man was fine as hell and time had done something good for him. This man standing in front of me wasn't the same Haze that used to get on my nerves. It couldn't be. Then, when I stared into his eyes I saw those same sincere eyes that I always looked into. The girl beside him sucked her teeth again and I could tell she was in her feelings. I wanted to pop her in the mouth just because she was tap dancing on my nerves.

"Give me a minute." He gently squeezed my shoulders, then turned to his girl. "Yo, let me holla at you real quick." He took her hand into his hands and led her to his whip.

I jogged up the stairs and looked at Meeka. "I had no clue you knew Haze like that." She smiled. "How do you know him?"

"He was my next door neighbor for years."

"Oh okay. I knew he used to live in your building, but I didn't think y'all knew each other like that," I smiled while looking at him talk to his girlfriend. "You got a man, and Whitney doesn't play when it comes to Haze." Meeka snapped me from my nasty thoughts about Haze.

"I'm not thinking about him like that. Like you said... I got a man," I choked out. Bridge was the last person that I was thinking about. After seeing Haze, it was Bridge, who?

"Your words are telling me one thing, but your actions are telling me something else." Meeka finished her wine cooler.

The front door opened and Kook stuck his head out. Soon as his eyes landed on Meeka, he gave her a head nod. She turned to say something to me and I held my hand up. I was all too familiar about that head nod. "Girl, save your breath and go be with your man. I'm about to head to the hotel anyway," I followed behind her so I could get my purse.

Meeka giggled like a school kid. From being around she

and Kook, I could tell he loved the hell out of his woman and there wasn't anything he wouldn't do for her. I loved how they joked and when it got serious about their daughter they were all about her. I could tell Kook never laid a hand on Meeka. He had respect for her. I wish I had the same thing waiting for me when I got back home. Bridge wouldn't know what respect was if it punched him in the face. Even then, he still wouldn't know what it was. I grabbed my purse while Meeka grabbed some water from the fridge.

"Call me later. With him being able to get our daughter down for a nap, we need this time." She damn near pleaded.

"I understand. I'm gonna start packing and trying to decide when the hell I'm going to head back home."

"Shoot me a text and let me know when you decide when you're going to head home." She told me and headed toward the steps.

I opened the door and walked right into Haze's chest. Looking up at him, I smiled and tried to get past him. "Where you going?"

"I need to go back to my hotel so I could pack and decide when I'm going back home. Saylor is going to meet me there too."

"You gonna leave and not bother to kick it with me before bouncing?" he faked like he was hurt.

Twirling my hair around my finger, I looked at him and smirked. "Your girlfriend doesn't seem too pleased with me being around you."

"Nah, she understands now. I explained that you're an old friend."

"Oh did you?"

"Word to my moms."

I snatched his phone out of his hands and programmed my

number into his phone. "Call me and we all can link before I leave."

He looked down at his phone. "Maryland? You moved out there."

I smiled. "Yes."

"We definitely gotta link before you bounce." He pulled me into a hug. I smelled his cologne and melted at the scent of his Fendi cologne. I knew it was Fendi because Bridge had the same one. For some reason, it smelled so much better on Haze.

"Alright. Make sure you call or text me," I winked and headed to my car. When I walked by his car, Whitney was in the front seat giving me the stink eye. Instead of paying her any attention, I hit the key fob, got behind the wheel, and headed back to the hotel.

"Traffic was crazy," Saylor said as she walked through the door of our hotel suite. She closed the door behind her and kicked her shoes off. "I thought you were going to be by Meeka's house?"

I had been back to my hotel for three hours and had sent Saylor about six text messages. She never told me where she was going, and I wasn't concerned. As far as I was concerned, she was a grown woman and I didn't need to keep tabs on her. I folded the shirt and placed it into my luggage and looked at Saylor.

"I've sent you about six damn text messages."

She held her phone up. "Phone died while I was heading here." She held up her dead phone. "Why are you packing?"

"I have to go back soon, Saylor. I can't just live in this hotel and hide from Bridge."

From the look on Saylor's face I could tell she was ready to have an argument about this right now. We've had fun since I've been here and we've connected in a way we haven't in a long time, however, that was because the subject of Bridge hadn't been brought up. Each time his name was brought up, I switched the subject. I already knew how she felt and I respected how she felt. Still, she couldn't expect me to just give up my entire life and never look back. It was unfair of her to expect that from me when I knew if the roles were reversed she wouldn't do the same.

"Why are you going back to him, Kenni? Last time you got away because of Juleena, what happens when he decides to bust your head open again?"

I sighed and tossed the pair of jeans I was folding into my bag. "There's not going to be a next time. I know what I have to do and this time away with you has given me strength."

"And what is that you have to do?"

"Tell Bridge that he needs to change his ways or I'm going to leave."

Saylor rolled her eyes and blew out a breath. "And that doesn't work when you say you're going to leave and you don't."

"I'm really going to leave. Hell, maybe I'll move to Virginia."

"Virginia? So, you wouldn't move back to New York? That's our home." She plopped down on the bed. "I really can't believe that you're going back."

"New York is your home... who do I have there? My mother is wherever she is, and we haven't spoken in years. My brothers are in Georgia. You're the only one in New York, Saylor."

"That should be enough for you to come back."

I picked the jeans up and sighed. "I have to go back home. The plan was to get away for the weekend and I've been here for a week," I shut the conversation down and Saylor knew not to bring it up again. I loved her and appreciated that she worried about me. It showed she cared, however, I had to live my life without her being upset each time I did something that she didn't like.

Meet me at the R&B lounge on Walnut Alley, I looked at the message from an unknown number. *It's Haze.* Just as I was about to reply asking who it was, his name popped up. I smiled.

"We've been arguing about me going home and I forgot to tell you what happened today," I broke the silence in the room. From Saylor's posture and look, I could tell she was thinking.

"What happened?" she stared at me.

"I ran into Haze."

Her face dropped as she continued to stare at me. "Haze? Haze, Haze?" she made sure that we were talking about the same person.

"Yes, and he says Hans is alive."

"Are you fucking with me?"

"No, I'm being serious," I giggled. "And he's not the same Haze," I fanned myself with my toiletries bag. "He pulled up pushing a black Bentley, dressed in designer shit with jewelry and his hair was braided."

"Who the fuck did he rob?" Saylor spoke more to herself than me.

I shrugged. "He's so different, yet he's the same," I sighed and took a seat in the chair. "He's fine as fuck," I made sure to add.

"Now that's something I didn't think I would ever hear you say," Saylor teased.

She was right. When we were younger, I always paid Haze no mind. In my head, he couldn't fund the lifestyle I was looking for. Even when he made all these promises, I never paid him any mind. I had men like Byron and Bridge who were handing me money like it grew on trees. Haze could barely feed himself without Hans being there to help him. So, how was he going to give me the world he always promised to give me? We were young and I should have been patient, yet, I couldn't afford to trust and wait on promises. I had to leave my mother's house and if I would have waited on Haze, I would have been getting my ass kicked for being me.

"You have to see him. He just sent me a text and told me we're going to kick it at a lounge."

Saylor lifted her eyebrow. "Kick it at the lounge? Exactly how much did I miss? You got his number and shit?"

"I actually gave him my number. He said he wanted to see you and kick it with me before I left to go back home."

"I'm excited like hell to see lil' Haze," she joked. Saylor was always the first person to point out that Haze liked me. Each time we were around each other she would always make him feel shy when she brought it up. Back then, I never paid it any mind. To me, Haze was my friend and neighbor; nothing more.

After I finished packing up all the clothes I had accumulated, I pulled out a quick chill outfit and went to shower. Saylor changed her clothes and did her hair while I was getting dressed. By the time I was fully dressed, she was done and we headed out. Instead of driving, we decided to call a cab since there was a chance we would be drinking tonight. As we sat in the back of the cab, I worried about seeing Haze again.

"Why you playing with your hands like this is a date?" Saylor teased me. "We're just kicking it," she reminded me and I calmed down. *Why was I so nervous?* It wasn't like we were going on a date or like it would be more than what we were. I would go back to Maryland and he would continue his life here in Virginia.

"You're right. It's just that.... You haven't seen him," I blushed and leaned my head on her shoulder. She quickly exited out of the text message screen and then rubbed my hair.

"I guess I'll be in for a treat tonight."

"Yep."

We arrived to the lounge and were welcomed right inside. Haze had told me that they were running late, so we headed to the bar to have a few drinks before they came. I had become this home body who hardly ever got drunk or had a drink. So, tonight I planned on having a few drinks so they could calm my nerves down. Saylor sat on the stool next to mine and crossed her legs while pecking away on her cellphone.

"Who are you texting?" I questioned. "Are you back dating again?"

She smiled. "Something like that. Please don't get all mushy either. I'm just dipping my feet in the water, that's all." She tried to convince me.

"From the way you're smirking while sending those messages, it seems like you're doing more than dipping in the water," I waved the bartender over.

"Why are you all in my business anyway?"

"Well, since you're always in my business I figured I'd return the favor," I laughed. "Can we have two long island iced teas and two shots of Hennessy?"

He nodded his head and went to grab our drinks. "I'm only in your business because I care about you, Kenni. The last thing I want is to open the newspaper and see you've been killed." She got serious and sat her phone down.

"Stop thinking like that. I'm telling Bridge my conditions and if he doesn't agree, I'm leaving," I promised her.

That was my plan. I planned on going home and letting Bridge know that I wasn't going to put up with his bullshit anymore. The sleeping around with his baby mamas, disrespect and abusive behavior wasn't something I was going to continue to put up with. I deserved better and if he wasn't going to give it to me, then I had to leave. I didn't give a damn how he felt, I had to go if he couldn't change his ways.

"I just worry about you, Kenni. I never want something to happen to you. You and Nana are the only family members that I have."

"I know. You guys are the only family that I have too." The bartender sat our drinks down and left to tend to the other patrons. "Let's take a shot," I held up mine and she grabbed hers.

"To spending more time together." We held up our drinks and cheered before downing them down. I put my shot glass down and grabbed my long island iced tea to chase the shot down.

"Definitely, we need to spend more time together," I agreed and continued to sip on my drink. I missed spending time with my best friend.

Saylor and Bridge didn't get along so she refused to come to our home, and even then, Bridge didn't want her in our house either. I was caught between two people I cared for and couldn't choose sides. While I loved Saylor, I also had to have a life of my own too. Just because she and Bridge didn't get along I couldn't just end things with him because that's what she wanted. Just like I didn't expect her to end any of her relationships for me. Out the corner of my eye, I noticed Haze and Hans walking toward us. Out of habit, I licked my lips and sucked my straw a little harder while watching him walk over to us. Just that quick, Saylor was back into her phone and sipping her drink, so she wasn't paying anyone any mind.

"I see you got the party jumping before we got here," Haze

hugged me and I looked over at Hans. "Don't act all shy now... you kept asking for this nigga."

Hans smirked and held his arms out. "What's fucking good, Kenni?" he pulled me into his big arms and kissed me on the head. "I missed the hell out of your grown ass." He kidded.

"Grown ass? Man, I'm grown," I punched him in the chest and hugged him again. Hans and Haze were practically twins. Haze resembled his brother, except, Hans had big doe shaped eyes and he kept a low cut, where Haze rocked his signature braids. Hans was also a couple inches taller than Haze too.

"I can see... I can see," he gave me a once over. Why big head over there acting like she didn't miss a nigga?" he pointed to Saylor who was now looking at us with a goofy grin on her face.

She quickly jumped out the chair and rushed into Han's arms. She hugged him just like I had hugged Haze earlier. She backed up and then punched him in the chest three times. "Why the hell would you leave and not tell anybody? We were worried about you." She punched him again.

"My bad. Shit was getting real in New York and we had to bounce. I couldn't stay there anymore. Niggas were being haters and trying to fuck up my money and end me." He pulled her back into his arms. "You forgive me?"

Saylor scrunched her face up and folded her arms. "I gotta think about it. Seriously, I'm happy that the both of you are good. Not a day went by that I didn't question myself about what happened to you both." She went over and hugged Haze.

"I should have reached out. A few times I was going to but stopped myself," Haze admitted.

I pinched him. "You could have at least answered my IM messages."

"Shit, throwback," Hans chuckled. "He tossed that shit

over the bridge when we were going into Jersey. I told him we needed a fresh start... for real."

Haze waved the bottle girl over. "Let me get a section for us," he told her.

She smiled at him and nodded. "I'll have one cleaned up for you right away." She went in the opposite direction.

"Damn, you got pull like that?"

"You can have any kind of pull when you own the shit." Haze laughed. "What you drinking on?" he grabbed my drink off the bar.

"Long island iced tea," I replied and climbed back on the stool.

I was glad that I decided to wear something comfortable and cute tonight. Tonight, I was dressed in a pair of skinny jeans, Gucci boots with a white T-shirt and purse that matched the boots. My hair was pulled back into a sleek ponytail and I had no makeup on.

"Still sipping that nasty shit years later."

"Boy, stop hating on my drink. Your bartender makes it really yummy too," I took another sip and crossed my legs.

Haze was eyeing me like a lion eyed a steak. I could tell he was enjoying the view from the way he kept licking his lips and leaned over my chair. "Mr. Regis, the section is ready," the same bottle girl came over and told us.

I grabbed my drink and we walked over to the section that already had bottles sitting in the ice bucket on the table. The vibe of the lounge was cool. I took a seat in the middle of the section and crossed my legs. Haze sat beside me and grabbed the bottle of champagne that was chilled in the bucket.

"What you been up to?"

I sipped my drink. What was I supposed to say? Life wasn't

great, although I looked good. I wasn't ready to tell him my business yet.

"I've been living life. What about you?"

"Shit, I been doing the same. I still can't believe I'm sitting here with you." He smirked and moved closer to me.

"I see you got a little wifey and stuff," I cut my eyes at him. Why was him having a girlfriend making me jealous? I guess I was so used to Haze always being stuck on me that I never thought he would date anyone else, even with his disappearing. It sounded silly, but it was how I thought.

"You saw her. Nothing on shorty is little," he joked.

"Boy bye... you need to quit."

"I'm fucking with you... me and her been rocking for a minute." Saylor and Hans were having their own conversation. So, me and Haze leaned back and had our own too. It felt good. At first, I was nervous and now it was like old times. We were all just kicking it and enjoying each other's company. This was just what I needed.

Two

Haze

"I TOLD you once you went out last night that you were going to be sleepy all day. We always go to the zoo on Saturdays," Whitney complained as she brushed her hair in the mirror.

I leaned up in the bed and I had a headache. Last night, I didn't mean to drink as much as I did. A few drinks and catching up with Kenni was the plan. Next thing I knew, we were ordering buckets of bottles and catching up on the old times. It wasn't until Kenni received the call about her cousin in law being in an accident that I realized that we shut the lounge down and it was after four in the morning. I never stayed out late anymore and always prided myself on being in the house before midnight. Whitney continued to pull her hair into a ponytail and give me an attitude. This was new to her. I was always home at night and she never had to call me over a dozen times to ask me when I would be home because I was always home. I understood what she felt and I could see why she had an attitude. Still, she couldn't be as mad because it wasn't something that I always did.

Pulling the covers off my body, I sat on the edge of the bed and looked over at her. "You take Brittany and go out and have a girls day. I'll catch up with y'all later and we'll go to dinner," I promised.

Whitney snapped her neck and turned to face me with her hand holding onto her ponytail. "Dinner? You're really going to blow us off for the weekend and then try and make it up with dinner?" she rolled her eyes.

"Why you doing all of this? It's hella early," I complained. Whitney knew how to piss me off early in the morning.

Every weekend I spent the day with Whitney and her daughter Brittany. Since I was busy all week, I dedicated the weekend to them both. Whitney knew I had to bring in the money and never complained about me working all week. She knew the weekend was dedicated to both she and Brittany. This was the first weekend since she moved in a year ago that I wasn't going to spend with them and she was acting like I never showed up or out for them during the weekends. I watched as she turned back around and finished fixing her hair with a pout on her face.

"Hazyyyy!" Brittany came running into our bedroom with her favorite teddy bear. Brit was four years old and she loved her some me.

"Brit Brat!" I kissed her on the cheeks and tickled her while she giggled in my ear.

Whitney finished her hair and watched me and Brittany playing with each other. I could tell she wanted to join in on the fun, but she was too into her feelings to admit that. I continued to play with Brittany while ignoring her mama's stares from across the room. She knew I hated when she was in her feelings and putting that infamous pout on her face. I hated to see her upset and always tried to avoid anything that would cause her to be upset with me. She was my love. My everything. So, why the fuck would I want to see her upset or stressing out?

"Mama is upset with me," I told Brittany, and she stopped playing and looked over at her mother. "I can't spend today with you girls. I have some things to do," I added.

Brittany put her sad face on and touched my face. "It's okay. Me and mommy will have fun together." She kissed me on the cheek and held onto my face.

I kissed her little hands and looked at Whitney. "Not fair, Haze."

"What you mean?"

"You know exactly what I mean. Using Brittany is not fair." She held her hand on her hips. Whitney used to be slim. From the pictures she showed me, shorty used to weigh around one hundred and fifty pounds soaking wet.

Now, she was still somewhat slim, but she had developed a body. I met her after she had Brittany, and I thanked God for that. Brittany had given her some ass, breast, and some hips. She stood around 5'4 with light brown skin and sandy brown hair that fell past her shoulders. I loved when she wet it and wore her natural curls. Shit was a turn on to me. Her juicy pink lips were always slathered with lip gloss and her big bright hazel eyes were always filled with hope and excitement when she saw me.

"I'm not using her. She understands and you're acting like you don't. One weekend. That's all I'm asking." Whitney sucked her teeth and grabbed her ringing cellphone off the vanity. I watched as she left the room and me and Brittany sat on the bed. "You look so pretty today, Britty Brat." Her black pig tails were neatly brushed and her coiled ponytail swung from side to side when she walked.

"Thank you, Hazy!" she smiled at me and hugged her teddy bear tighter. I watched as she jumped down from the bed and left the room.

I leaned back in the bed and checked my messages. Hans had sent me a few messages and a few other niggas sent me some too. I put my phone down when Whitney came back into the room. She held her phone in one hand and Brittany's overnight bag in the other.

"Rod wants to come and pick Brit up for the weekend. His baby shower is tomorrow," she informed me. "You know I didn't want her to go and now I literally have no excuse as to why she can't come," she sulked.

I leaned up in the bed and held my hand out. "Come here." She walked over and plopped down on the bed beside me. I kissed her lips and rubbed her thighs. "She's excited about her new baby brother. Just let her go."

I knew it was more to the story as to why Whitney was pressing me about not spending the weekend with them. She was never like this when it came to me having to handle business. Brittany's father was having a baby by her God mother. Whit was hurt like shit when she found out that her cousin was having a baby by the same nigga she used to cry to her about. It was fucked up and I had to hear her cry about it for months. I heard about Rod before I even met Whitney. He wasn't happy for new players to enter what he thought was his game. There was some beef there, but I lived by the rule that if you didn't address that shit, it wasn't real. His ass never came to me about it, so the shit didn't matter to me nor Hans. When I met Whitney, he called himself trying to press Whit about being careful with me. Knowing that I was digging his baby mom's back out and being a step-father to Brittany pissed his ass off and I knew it. Whit went to court when they first broke up and they shared custody. He had Brittany Every other week. This week happened to be Whitney's week and she was adamant about Brit not going to the baby shower.

"You mean her new baby cousin? I can't put my stamp of approval on this. Malika knew what she was doing. Like, how could she?" she vented, like she always did when this topic came up.

"Babe, I know the shit is still fresh, but you need to let the shit go. The baby got one foot out her pussy... There's nothing you can do to stop whatever they over there doing."

She got up from the bed and stalked out the room. Whenever this shit came up it brought tension into our crib. I understood she was upset and this shit was foul on all levels, however, why the fuck was I paying for what Rod's ass did? Instead of laying in the bed, I grabbed my phone and dialed my brother and went into the bathroom to brush my teeth and shit.

"You just now getting up?" he grunted into the phone.

I laughed because his ass was working out like he did every morning. "Yeah. Whitney beefing because I came home early in the morning."

"I knew she would. You spoiled her ass with all that family time and no late hours shit," he replied.

"That's what happens when you get into a relationship, nigga," I laughed and put toothpaste onto my toothbrush.

Hans prided himself on always being single. Since we left New York, he had only been involved in one serious relationship. After it ended, he just played the field. You would never find him involved with the same female more than twice. He was a one and done type of nigga, and if you had real good pussy he would come back for seconds before deleting your number out his phone. His focus was always on the money and making sure we were always making money. He never wanted to go back to being broke, so he focused on what was consistent in his life; money.

"Yeah, you keep telling yourself that. You got Whitney spoiled by you always being there. Then, you playing daddy and shit." Hans liked Whitney; however, he didn't trust her. Once he found out that she was Rod's baby mama, all bets were off with him getting to know her better or trusting her. "That relationship shit makes you weak."

"Nigga, from the way you were all over Saylor last night, I can't tell."

He chuckled. "You know Saylor always been my little baby... it was good seeing her last night," I could hear the smile in his voice.

Hans had always kept his eyes on Saylor back in the hood. He loved how she was about her business and wasn't chasing after dick like Kenni. "Yeah, she looked like she could be more than your little baby... nigga, she was all on your lap and shit," I recalled the events of last night.

"Shit, we were kicking it and having drinks. I didn't say shit when you were whispering all in Kenni's ear."

I smirked and looked out the bathroom to see if Whitney was anywhere near. Hans was on speaker and his ass was being mad loud. "Shut your loud ass up. I got you on speaker and I didn't tell Whit who I was with last night," I closed the bathroom door and started washing my face.

"You don't want to be in the dog house, huh?"Anyway, I know Saturdays are your family days so hit me when you're free."

"Brit is going over her father's crib, so I'm free... you trying to link?"

"Yeah. We need to convince Kook's crazy ass that he needs to stay out here and not move back to the city. Pops never had that plan when he handed everything over to us."

Kook was our half-brother. Our father had reached out to Hans and told him that he wanted to meet the both of us. At first, Hans didn't think we needed to meet him. He left our moms to raise us and battle cancer alone. He kept the shit to himself and put it off for an entire year before he entertained us going down there. Then, he got shot and we had to breeze, so our pops welcomed us to Virginia with open arms. Apparently, our pops was getting it and was a well-known Kingpin in Virginia and was running shit. Him and my moms separated because she refused to move from New York. He apologized about how he could have reached out and been there. Still, none of that mattered because he wasn't there and it was something I couldn't forgive. We found out that he was dying and he wanted his three sons to take over the family business. Here we were sitting in day old clothes and Hans with a blood stained shirt in the foyer of this nigga's mansion. All bets about him not being there went out the window and we got to work.

I believed my father really felt bad and regretted not being there for all of his sons. Although Kook was from Virginia, he wasn't in his life either. On his death bed, he cried about receiving forgiveness from me and my brothers. Hans and Kook was able to forgive and I wasn't. I couldn't forget about my mother battling cancer, trying to raise two boys and working a full time job. Everything in my heart couldn't forgive him off the fact that he was dying. Where was he when my mother was on her death bed worried about what was going to happen to her sons? The woman didn't give a damn that she was about to die. She was worried about if me and Hans would be alright since we had no family. I held his hand and told him it wasn't something that I could forgive. I prayed with him and he died while holding my hand. Seeing my brother be shot by the same niggas that he hit the block for was enough to turn me into a savage. My father hadn't been dead an hour and I got right to work. I couldn't forgive him, still, that didn't mean I wouldn't give it my all to make sure all he built continued to grow.

"Yeah. I'll meet you over there."

"Man, you in your head again? That's the only time you get all short on words."

All I could do is laugh because we knew each other so well. "I guess you could say that."

"About Kenni? I know how you felt about her back home." He was right. I did love Kenni and wanted to give her the world. After all these years, that feeling didn't waver. Even with not seeing her for years, she still had that same hold over my heart.

"Stop playing. Plus, she still with that nigga Bridge."

"I been hearing that nigga's name... it's getting closer and closer to out here." Hans mentioned. "You could tell she into you now. Probably because you got some money. Kenni always been a shallow ass fast ass."

"That's the thing. She's different now. I don't know what it is, but she's real different," I sat on the edge of the tub.

When Whitney walked into the bathroom I took the phone off speaker. "Yeah, that's what you say. I know Kenni back then couldn't give you three solid seconds. And, she gave you a whole night last night."

"Whatever. I'll see you in an hour or so," I ended the call with him.

Whitney grabbed all Brittany's hair products and put them in her overnight bag. "Who were you with last night?" Whitney randomly asked.

"Me and Hans were chilling at the lounge with Kenni and Saylor," I could have lied and told her some story about me and Hans chilling. What would that do? Me and Kenni were catching up and nothing happened.

She spun around so fast I got a headache. "The same bitch that ran and jumped on you?" she questioned me, even though she knew the answer. "And you came in late and didn't feel the need to tell me about it?"

I stood up and walked back into the bedroom. "I'm a grown ass man, Whitney. The fuck I gotta tell you about everything I'm doing?"

"Because I'm your fucking girl. If I was hanging out with a nigga you didn't like, you would have a heart attack," she accused.

"You don't like Kenni why?"

She shrugged her shoulders. "I could see the lust all in her eyes."

"She got a nigga."

"And? That don't stop these hoes. If she was really a friend you would have kept in contact. I don't want you around her." She pointed her finger at me.

Whitney didn't give a fuck who a woman was, she never wanted them around me. I think it stemmed from the fact that her cousin was expecting a baby with her baby daddy. I understood her trust issues, yet, she couldn't put that shit on me.

"I'm a grown ass man, Whitney. You not 'bout to tell me what to do. Kenni is the homie. Nothing more." I got up and left the bathroom. She knew not to follow me when I got pissed off, so she let me leave in peace.

☆ ☆ ☆

I hit the locks and walked up the steps into Kook's crib. Meeka's car was gone so she was probably somewhere shopping with their daughter. All Meeka's ass did was shop, suck Kook dry, and take care of their home. Whitney called herself trying to take advice from her a few times and I had to shut that shit down. Meeka was cool peoples, but I didn't want my girl being her. I loved what she did for her man and family, but that wasn't what I wanted. Meeka did whatever Kook wanted and followed his lead because he provided for their family. I liked my women to be vocal. Yeah, I liked to provide, but at the same time I wanted a woman who wasn't afraid to put me in my place. Don't get me wrong, Meeka had mouth on her and argued with Kook when she felt strong about something. Other than that, she did whatever Kook wanted and never questioned his moves.

"About time you showed up. The fuck were you doing? Fucking?" Kook pulled on his cigarette and kicked his feet up.

"Nah, Whitney had an attitude and I had to make sure we were good before I dipped out." I plopped down on the couch across from him, next to Hans.

"She always got an attitude about something," Hans made sure to add his two cents. The fact that she wasn't his favorite person made it easier for him to comment on her.

I grabbed the freshly rolled blunt from the ashtray and lit it before taking a pull and leaning back. "Why y'all in my business. I had to make sure my girl is good."

"You and shorty from yesterday had nothing to do with it?" Kook raised his eyebrow. "Meeka told me how she jumped into your arms while Whitney stood right there."

"We cool peoples. That's all. Whit is being dramatic."

"Is she?" he countered.

"Yeah. Kenni got her own situation going on... I'm not worried about her, and she's not worried about me."

"According to big bro, you used to chase her around in the hood back in the day."

I pulled on my blunt and looked at Hans. "Snitch ass nigga."

"You think I'm going to believe that no feelings came back from seeing and kicking it with her last night?"

I would be lying if I said I didn't feel shit for Kenni. I did feel something and while hanging with her, it was like no time had passed between us both. She had matured a lot and material shit wasn't that important to her anymore. I guess because she had everything she had been trying to work toward back then so there was no need for her to be materialistic anymore. Either way, I could tell she wasn't the same Kenni, and she had changed for the best.

"Can we focus on why the fuck we came over here?" I switched the subject. I didn't know when the fuck my life had become a topic for discussion.

Hans leaned up on the couch and looked over at Kook, who continued to puff on his cigarette carelessly. "You really going to move to New York?"

"Yeah."

"For what? I'm not going to say there's no money in New York, but why the fuck uproot your family and shit?"

"There's money up there to be made. Why we sitting back and collecting money here when we could get more."

"Greed," I spoke up.

Kook looked over to me. "Fuck you mean?"

"We're blessed here. Nobody hurting for money and we don't have nobody gunning at our head in New York. Pops gave us the key, but we opened the door with that shit. Why go into unknown territory being greedy?"

When me and Hans fled from New York, I was scared as fuck. My brother was nearly killed, and he was the only person I had in this life. Was I afraid to admit that I was scared? Hell nah. I was terrified. Then, I grew up and realized those niggas that tried to end my brother bled just like me. I wasn't afraid to head back to New York; I just didn't see the need. We were making good money here. Why fuck that up? I knew New York could bring us more money, but why? Kook was so obsessed with getting and wanting more that he refused to see that this move wasn't for right now. I'm not saying I wouldn't be open to heading back home in the future, however, I wasn't in that place right now.

"Yeah, but what about having more? We live decent, but we could live how pops lived. You saw that mansion he was living in."

"All I saw was a man having to keep putting his life on the line to continue with his appearance. Pops looked like the big man on campus but look where his mansions are; foreclosed," Hans said.

My father made it look like he was the man on the surface. Under all of that, the man owed everybody and his mama, his mansion was in foreclosure and he was on the verge of losing it all. If it wasn't for me and my brothers coming in and turning shit around, he would have lost it all. Moving here I thought we would instantly be rich and not have to struggle, but that wasn't the case. Meeting a father that has a mansion meant that I was about to be rich. Wrong. We didn't go without meals, but we sure as hell wasn't driving in the newest whips and having the fly clothes. We had to damn near sell anything that my father did own to pay back his debts, and make sure we could afford to reup on work. The shit wasn't easy and I hated when anybody thought we moved and had it good. It was the reason I appreciated everything I had now. Shit wasn't handed to us.

"Yeah, and if we wanna keep making this money we need to expand up north. New York niggas really know how to get it. I'm still confused why the fuck y'all even came down here."

"Because I would have been visiting him in a fucking grave. I get you idolize New York niggas, but you need to be smart. Those same niggas that you're idolizing are the same niggas that'll shoot you in the head and console your baby moms at your funeral. All I'm saying is chill on the whole New York thing for another year. We're about to start working with a new supplier and I want to get in good before taking in more."

As hard headed as Kook was, he knew that we both were right. His sudden itch to expand was admirable, however, we needed to be smart with how we moved and continued to build in the south. "Plus, we've been doing good in Atlanta... everything is looking like a go there," I reminded him.

"Yeah, ight. I'll listen for now..." Kook flicked his ashes and put his cigarette out before heading upstairs.

"Stay out your feelings, nigga. Ain't no money there!" Hans yelled behind him and we both laughed.

He was the youngest and the most eager to make moves. I knew we held him back and babied him because we wanted to make sure he moved smart. "We can't hold him back forever," I told Hans. "He's going to want to make moves on his own someday."

Me and Kook were a year apart. While I thought about shit before I did it, Kook was quick to fly off the handle and then think about shit later. "And when he does, he'll be on his own. Pops handed this shit to all of us so we need to stay together.

Money is good and life is good. No need to fuck with it." He put his feet up on the coffee table and relaxed his arms.

I stood up and shook my head. "Bet. I'll holla at y'all later," I told him and headed out. When me and Whitney were fighting I hated the shit, so I was heading to go and make peace with my woman so I didn't have to have her slamming plates around the crib.

Three

Bridge

I STARED across the room at Kenni sitting by Juleena's bedside. She was holding Juleena's hand and refused to look over at me. Since she had come storming into the hospital room she hadn't bothered to look over at me. My blood boiled because I wanted to know what the fuck she had been up to. Since she dipped, I hadn't had no pussy. I was too concerned with where the fuck her ass was at to be worried about sliding up in India or Mercedes's pussy. Both of them were pissing me the fuck off with their nagging ass behavior.

"Even with you being in an accident, you're still beautiful," Kenni said and kissed Juleena's hand.

Juleena had got hit bad and it was a miracle that she was even alive. Her car was totaled and she had passed out once her head hit the steering wheel. They had to cut her out the car and transport her to the nearest hospital in Virginia. When I got the call, I called my aunt and we drove to the hospital together. My aunt had been so concerned with Juleena and making sure the boys were straight that it left me to call Kenni and let her know. She ignored my damn calls until she finally decided to answer and even then, she sounded like she had been drinking and was in a club. When she came in here, I could tell she was out when I called her. Even if the sound of her voice and her background wasn't evident enough.

"Thank you, babe... I just want to get back on my feet and home." She tightly squeezed Kenni's hand.

"The doctor said that he'll discharge you this week. I don't want you rushing and shit to get back home. You need to heal." Brix stood over her and kissed her on the lips. "We could have lost you."

"Kenni, I'm about to head out... do you need me to come by and pick you up to drop you back to your car?" Saylor popped her head into the room.

"She good. I'll drop her by her car when we're done here," I told Saylor.

Saylor's disrespectful ass looked right past me into Kenni's eyes. "What do *you* wanna do, Ken?"

Kenni looked at Saylor and shrugged her shoulders. "I guess Bridge can drop me back off to my car. I still have to get my things anyway." Saylor rolled her eyes. "Call me when you make it home."

"Ight." Saylor closed the door back. I watched as Brix watched Saylor and licked his lips. When he saw me looking, he tried to change his facial expression. I knew that nigga loved Saylor and all these years he tried to make it work with Juleena, even though his heart wasn't with her. I didn't doubt that he loved her and the boys. He just wasn't in love with Juleena and her boys were forced upon him.

"You good, Brix?" I looked at him.

"Yeah. I'm straight," he replied and sat down in his chair.

Either Juleena was good at pretending or she had no clue that this nigga wasn't in love with her. Like I told her, I hated when she inserted herself into me and Kenni's business, so I wasn't about to insert myself into theirs.

"It's noon and you've been here since before five. I'm fine and mama isn't going to let anything happen to me," she joked.

"You're damn right." My aunt Jessica said while crocheting in the corner. "Go get some rest, baby," she touched Kenni's back.

Juleena and my aunt Jessica took a special liking to Kenni since I brought her home to meet them. As the years went by, the bond only got closer. To the fact that Jessica refused to talk to me because I put my hands on Kenni.

"Okay." Kenni looked me in the eyes, then looked over at Brix. "Will you drive me back to Richmond?"

"Kenni, don't make me punch you in the h—"

"I can't control what kind of twisted shit goes on under your roof, but I can control what goes on here, Maurice." She pointed her crochet needle at me.

Kenni quickly left the room and I motioned for Brix to sit back down, then followed Kenni out into the hallway.

"When will you change?" she laughed to herself and paced the floor. "Your cousin could have just lost her life and you're sitting here threatening me. I'm stupid to believe that you would change," she spoke to herself.

I put my hands in my pocket and leaned on the wall. "I fucked up, Ken."

"You tell me this all the time, Maurice. I'm tired of going through this with you and hearing the same weak ass apology." Whenever Kenni hung around Saylor, she became this strong ass woman that felt like she could hold her own when it came to me. Saylor put a battery into her back that now I was forced to stomp out her back and humble her ass again.

"And I'm telling you now that I fucked up. This time apart was good for us," I lied. "You needed space and it gave me time to think about how much you love and do for me. Waking up and not hearing you hum while in the laundry room or doing your hair really fucked me up."

I could see her expression soften. "Do you think I want to go away each time we argue? I need you to understand that this relationship isn't always only about you. I matter too."

"I hear you."

"Good. Can you drop me off to grab my things and my car?"

I nodded. "Yeah. Can you do me a favor?"

"What?"

"Give me a hug and kiss... Maybe act like you missed your man," I held my arms out and she smiled before walking into my arms and lifting her head so I could kiss her on the lips.

Despite all the shit that I put Kenni through or all the shit we've been through, I loved the shit out of her. No matter how mad she made me, I could never see us ending. We were in this shit for life and I would never willingly allow her to leave or let another nigga swoop in and take my spot.

"I did miss you," she admitted.

"I missed you too... don't do that again, ight?"

"Don't give me a reason to," she countered and started walking to the elevator. I bit the inside of my cheek because she thought this was going to be her new thing whenever she was upset.

Kenni's hotel was thirty minutes from the hospital. I had asked Juleena what she was doing in Virginia and she lied and told me some bullshit excuse about how she had a meeting with a lady that was going to provide her shops with raw Indian hair. I could tell Juleena was lying because she couldn't look me in the eyes and she always stared me in the eyes when she spoke to me. Brix had no clue because he didn't know shit about Juleena, even after being with her for years. He believed she was here on business when I knew it was something else. Instead of poking her about the matter, I allowed her to rock and acted as if I believed her, when I didn't.

"Who was paying for all of this?" I looked around the hotel suite. Shit, I knew for sure I wasn't paying for this shit.

"Um, Saylor paid for it. It was part of our girl's weekend," she stuttered as she grabbed more shit from the bathroom and packed it into her bag. "This was well needed. I missed Saylor so much." She tried to talk more to avoid me asking more questions about who paid for the room.

"So Juleena was staying here before she got into her accident?"

"No," she waved me off, then stopped short when she realized she had fucked up. "Juleena was going to come, but she decided to spend time with Brix. I guess she was coming to see me when she got into the accident," I could tell she was lying right through her teeth.

"Oh, word?"

"Yeah, I was upset when she pulled out." She continued to pack her shit into the bag. "What did you do while I was away?"

"Spent time with the kids," I lied. "Was worried about you too."

She turned around and offered me a weak smile. "I'm sorry for leaving and not answering your calls. I should have let you know I was good." She came and sat beside me.

I took Kenni's hand in mine and kissed it. "We need to do better and you need to stop thinking running off is going to solve everything."

She looked me in the eyes and sighed. "I know. It's not going to solve everything. I need you to put your baby mama's in check, Maurice. They both feel like they have more rights than I do. They show up to our home or call you all times of the night, even when it has nothing to do with the kids." She brought up.

Both Mercedes and India didn't want me and Kenni to be together. I knew they were upset about me choosing her over them. When it came to Kenni, she brought something different to the table. She wasn't Mercedes or India. Niggas had ran through them. With Kenni, everybody wanted her and couldn't have her. Having someone that everybody wanted was a fucking perk. All the niggas that worked for me stared at Kenni like she was a goddess and knew they couldn't touch her. I loved that niggas thought I was the luckiest nigga in the world. That feeling was one that I never got tired of.

"When we get home, I'll tell them to come to the crib and we both can sit down and talk to them."

She quickly turned toward me with a smile on her face. "Seriously?"

"Yeah, I wanna make you happy. If setting boundaries with them is what needs to happen, then that's what we have to do." I kissed her on the lips. The last thing I wanted to do was invite Mercedes and India over to the crib. Between the both of them,

I knew the shit wouldn't end right. Especially with Kenni laying down the rules. According to Kenni, she didn't know that I was still fucking the both of them.

"Babe, all I want is for us to work. I'm not trying to spend all the time arguing, but they both need to know that I'm not going nowhere."

I pulled Kenni onto my lap and kissed her on the neck. "Word? You're not going nowhere? Promise?"

"You know I love your stupid ass... I can't never leave you," she kissed me on the lips. "You need to learn how to control your anger. I'm tired of you putting your hands on me, Maurice." She stared into my eyes.

While looking into her eyes, I felt bad for putting my hands on her. Kenni was the only person who brought that kind of anger out of me. She made me angry and I couldn't control what happened next. It didn't help when she opened that smart ass mouth and taunted me. Plenty of times I had tried to walk away and Kenni was right there taunting me and making me put my hands on her.

"I'm going to do better. You don't deserve that shit that I do and I'm going to be better. I want to marry you, Kenni."

She looked skeptical because I always told her that shit when I fucked up, so I wasn't surprised that she didn't believe me. On my mama, I really wanted to marry Kenni and give her my babies. I wanted Kenni to have my seeds too and being that I caused her to lose her last pregnancies, I wanted to make shit right between us.

"You say that all the time." She rubbed my face. "I just want us to be better. I can't keep putting up with this, babe. Next time, I'll leave and I won't come back." She threatened like that shit would ever happen. I would kill Kenni before I let her leave me and be happy with someone else.

"I promise. I'm going to be better. I got you," I promised and we kissed. I watched her get the rest of her shit together before she checked out from the hotel and I helped her to her car. Once she got in the car, she followed me home. My dick was busting through my jeans at the thought of fucking Kenni in our bed. My baby mamas and kids wasn't about to hear from me for a few days. I had to make sure Kenni was good before I dipped back out into the streets.

Four

Saylor

IT HAD BEEN a week since I had been home and I had heard from
Kenni twice. Each time I called, she told me she was busy and
would call me back. I worried about her and she knew I did. The
last thing I wanted was for her to head back home with Bridge. I
didn't trust that nigga as far as I could throw him. Kenni always
did what she wanted and didn't give a damn what anybody had to
say, which pissed me off. Spending time with just the two of us felt
like old times. She didn't have to answer to Bridge and we did
whatever we wanted. We had so many deep talks about how she
wanted to be single and move into her own apartment. Kenni had
never lived on her own or provided for herself. She moved right
out of her mama's house and right in with Bridge. Bridge had
always been the one who provided for her. Kenni didn't know
what it was like to get up and work for the things she wanted. It
was the main reason she put up with Bridge and his bullshit. She

was afraid to provide for herself and have to pay her own bills, and work for what she needed. I understood her fear, well at least I tried to. I couldn't understand how she would rather get beat instead of getting out and working so she could get away from him.

Hanging out with Haze and Hans was like the old days. I didn't realize how much I missed the both of them. Seeing Kenni and Haze's chemistry let me know that no time had passed between the both of them. I knew Haze had always loved Kenni and she never gave him the time of day. With her seeing how much he changed and how he was getting money, I knew that was something that made her even entertain him for the entire night. I had always had a small crush on Hans and hanging with him further proved that. That man was about making his money and being him. I never had to question if he was being real with me, because he spoke his mind. The entire night we sat, drank, and talked about the past. He asked me about Darren and I told him that he was locked up, but we still kept in contact. I could tell that there was something between the both of us, but I think he was hesitant. Hans had always been a playboy and messed with different chicks. He was never known to settle down with just one, so I wasn't surprised. My phone deterred me from my thoughts. When I looked at the name, I sighed.

"Hey," I answered and leaned back in my chair. I stirred the spoon around in my tea and looked out the window.

"What's good? How are you?" Brix questioned.

"I'm good. You?"

"It's been real busy around here. That's why I haven't been able to hit you up," he explained.

"You don't need to explain yourself. How is Juleena doing?"

"She's doing better. Still can't get around by herself... she has surgery coming up on her spine."

As much as I couldn't stand Juleena I never wanted her to hurt the way she was. "Oh."

I heard him close a door in his background before he spoke again. "I miss you," he admitted.

"Brix, it's best we continue to go about our lives. You have a lot going on at home and I—"

"I don't want to hear that shit, Saylor," he cut me off. "Don't do this to me," he pleaded with me.

Hearing him plead did something to my body. "Let me call you another time. I have something I'm doing right now," I lied and quickly ended the call.

I placed my phone down and leaned back in the chair. If I would have known bumping into Brix weeks ago would cause all of this, I would have never went to the soul food restaurant. Although I bowed out when we bumped into each other, he reached out to me on Facebook. I ignored him for a while until I couldn't anymore. He wrote me every morning and night until I finally replied with my number. I told him I was going to be in Virginia and if he wanted to link, he could meet me there. I was able to slip away so Kenni didn't ask too many questions and we found a coffee shop and sat down to talk. Brix admitted how much he loved me and how he made a mistake by picking Juleena over me. I wanted to believe him; I really did. Still, I couldn't believe him because he was still with her. How could you be with someone you claimed you weren't in love with?

"I'm going to head to the market to get some food for dinner," my nana told me. She knew how I felt about her driving and going out alone. I tried hard not to treat her like a baby, but I couldn't help it. She was all I had left besides Kenni, and I'd be damned if something happened to her.

"I'll come with you. I need to get some fresh air," I offered. Soon as I saw her turn her lips up, I knew she was upset that I offered to come.

"Saylor, the only reason I moved in here was because you begged me to move in with you. I had the cancer and I did need the help. I'm fine now and you're still treating me like a baby," she scolded me. "I'm a grown woman and I can go and handle getting groceries alone," she turned and walked out of the kitchen.

I laughed to myself because I acted just like my grandmother. It was the reason I was so independent. Esma loved to do things on her own and she had been doing things on her own for years. It was the reason she never dated and claimed she never had time for a man. I always wanted to be like my grandmother. She was so strong and never waited for anybody. Yet, I saw how she lived alone and didn't have love. She claimed my love was the only love she needed. I wanted love. For a while I had fought it, but I wanted to be loved. It had always been me and nana, and for once I wanted to have someone who loved me. Darren wasn't the answer. I put money on his books and visited him occasionally because I felt bad. He had looked out for me in the past so I was doing the same. Darren had a wife and kids, and I wasn't trying to be second again.

On the other hand, Brix had Juleena and no matter how much he tried to convince me that he wasn't in love with her, she lived in his home and he was helping to raise her kids. Kenni never liked to talk about Juleena whenever we were around because she knew how I felt. A few times she let it slip that she and Brix were so happy, or how he surprised her with a trip to the Bahamas for her birthday. That didn't sound like he didn't love her to me. It sounded like he was in love and wanted to have his cake and eat it too. I looked at my phone and picked it up to dial Hans. The phone rang for a few before he picked up and I heard his deep voice on the other end.

"What's good? I didn't think I was going to hear from your ass." He chuckled into the phone, which caused me to giggle.

"What makes you say that? I told you I would hit you when I got home."

"It take you a week to make it home?" he countered.

I smiled and held the phone to my cheek. "I had a lot of things going on that I had to handle. What are you up to?"

"In the bed 'bout to play with my dick."

"You're joking, right?"

"Hell nah... I gotta handle this stiffy. Unless you trying to come handle it for me." The thought of fucking Hans sounded tempting, since I hadn't had sex in a while.

"I'm sure you have enough chicks willing to handle that for you."

The phone grew quiet.

"I do... none of them could handle it like I know you can."

I bit down on my bottom lip. Me and Hans had never had sex or even made it that far. Our flirts were innocent back then. I was too concerned on getting out the hood and he was too. In a perfect world, we would have probably been something. Except the world wasn't perfect and we were trying to get out of our situation rather than worry about trying to be together.

"You don't know what I can handle so how you figure? Anyway, I called to see how you were doing?" It was half the truth. I was bored as hell and had nothing better to do. Brix was being way too clingy and Darren was in the hole for doing something stupid.

"How about you show me?"

"Hans, I'm going to hang up on your ass," I laughed.

"Ight... I'm good though. How are you?"

I sighed. "Bored."

"I thought you had businesses and shit. How you bored when you got businesses?" When we were at the lounge, we talked about everything. I told him about how I owned a few businesses in New York. He told me how he was about to open this restaurant.

"I pay people to handle my business so I don't have to."

"Pull up on me."

"Boy, that's six hours away. Who you think about to drive that long?"

He chuckled. "You right... I would pull up, but I got some shit I have to handle here. We need to work on when we're going to see each other... again."

"We'll figure it out."

"When's the next time you going to see Kenni? I heard she in Maryland now." He brought up. I wish I knew the next time I was going to see Kenni. Whenever Bridge was involved, we never linked like we used to. Hell, she never answered her phone so we could talk. Each time I tried to pop up, it was always a problem. I let her control when we would see each other.

"Kenni has her own life going in Maryland so I don't pop in like I used to... You know, to give her space," I lied.

"I hear that.... Let me make a call and I'm gonna hit you right back," he told me.

"K," I ended the call and then carried myself up to my bedroom.

As much as I loved being alone, it was something that I was starting to hate. I hated being alone and I wondered when it changed. When did I crave the company of a man? I could never be bothered with a man. Once Darren fucked me over, I told myself I would never be vulnerable like that again. Then Brix came along. He came along and made me feel again. He made me want to be loved and he showed me what it was like to be loved. He broke my heart too. So, as much as I wanted love and to be loved, it was easier to close myself off from love. Soon as I closed my eyes, my phone started ringing. I smiled when it was Hans. Maybe he did have to call someone and wasn't brushing me off.

"Yes," I yawned into the phone.

"Now you sound like you're going to sleep."

I giggled. "Actually, I'm lying in my bed right now."

"Get dressed."

"Huh?"

"Head over to the address that I'm sending you right now."

I leaned up in the bed. "Hans, what in the world are you talking about?" I was so confused.

"I wanna see you. Head to the address that I sent to you and I'll see you in less than an hour." He ended the call.

I opened my text messages and saw the address that he had sent me. Ripping the covers off my legs, I went to my computer in my office and typed the address into Google. I laughed when I saw it was a private airport.

An airport. What the hell?

I'm a nigga that puts action behinds his words. Get used to it shorty.

Omg

Call me when you get there. He responded back and I sighed and leaned back in my office chair.

☆

A private jet was waiting for me when I arrived. After getting the clearance, we headed into the sky and was touching down in Virginia in under an hour. I tried to bring my nana with me and she refused so I grabbed some clothes and then caught a cab to the airport. The pilot was heading to the hanger and I sat in the jet nervous as hell. I mean, who the hell charters a private jet in under ten minutes? Especially for me. The flight attendant came over to me and smiled.

"I hope the flight was to your liking."

"It was. Thank you so much," I replied and took the seat belt off. I grabbed my Chanel bag and stood up. She held my small duffle bag and I walked down the steps. Hans was waiting. He was leaning on a black Rolls Royce waiting for me.

Hans was fine as ever. He resembled his brother; however, he was a tad bit darker and he didn't have hair like Haze. His hair was cut low and his waves were so deep that he and the Atlantic ocean could be cousins. His lips were thick, pink and juicy. I stared into his dark brown bedroom eyes. I could tell he had smoked before coming to pick me up. He wore a pair of distressed jeans, white T-shirt and a pair of construction timberlands.

"This was too damn much," I said. It was the only thing I could think of to say. I rehearsed on the jet what I would say and how I would say it. None of that came to my head when I finally laid eyes on him.

"Nah, it wasn't nothing much." He walked around to the passenger side of the car and held the door open for me. I slid inside and looked at the car.

I was making more than I had ever made, but, I wasn't making Rolls Royce money. He walked over to the pilot and peeled some money off and handed it to him. Then, he grabbed my duffle bag from the flight attendant and put it in the backseat before jumping into the driver's seat.

"You really getting it, huh?" he smirked and pulled away from the jet. "I need to check into my hotel," I added.

Hans just told me to come to the airport. I had no clue what he had planned, and I didn't want to assume I was going to stay at his place, so I booked a hotel for myself. "Hotel? You wilding. If I invited and flew you to me, you gonna stay at my crib," he told me.

"You got enough room for me at your place? I'm not trying to be up in your place and you got your hoes in and out," I made that clear before canceling my hotel room. "I'm not trying to be uncomfortable."

"Same ass Saylor," he chuckled to himself. "Shorty, if I invited you to my crib that means you're special. I got a condo for the chicks I fuck around with. Nobody comes to my crib," he explained.

"Oh, you a baller like that, huh?"

"Deadass," he continued to drive.

He was chewing a piece of gum and the way his jawline flexed was enough for me to sit on his face. "I'm still trying to get over the fact that you sent a jet for me. Is that your jet?"

"Hell nah. I would never spend money on a damn jet. With fueling that shit and storage fees to keep it stored, niggas could have that. I'm cool with a nigga that owns one, and he happened to be in New York so I asked him to use it and tossed him a few dollars."

"Nigga must have wanted to see me bad, huh?" I snickered.

He looked over at me and then turned his attention back to the road. "Word." My heart started beating fast as shit when I heard him say word. "You know me and you know I'm not a nigga that baby foots around shit," he started.

"Oh, trust I know."

"We always had some kind of connection and we never acted on that shit. Mainly because you were out there doing you, and I wasn't trying to get caught up at the time," he admitted.

"Did we have some kind of connection, or did you just want to fuck? Help me understand," I joked with him.

He laughed. "I wanted to do that too, but I never was going to just fuck and dip on you. Which is why I never took it that far with you."

Me and Hans always flirted and once at a mutual friend's birthday party we almost took it all the way there. I kissed him and we were about to go inside and find an empty room, but he stopped. He made some dumb ass excuse and dipped down the staircase. I figured that he didn't like me the way I liked him and I left it alone. After that, we kept it to head nods or awkward side hugs.

"Is that the excuse you're going to go with? You remember at Kima's party when you ran down the stairs after giving me some bullshit excuse."

"I would have fucked the shit out of you that night and had you opened. I knew me and Haze were going to dip soon and I didn't want to take it there with you."

"I guess I should be flattered, huh?"

"You should be. I could have dogged that shit out and been out... If we were meant to meet again then God would make it happen."

I continued to look out the window. That night he gave me that excuse and left, I was upset. I didn't want to tell anybody because I was the girl every nigga always wanted. Never the one who got turned down. We continued to drive until we pulled into a subdivision with big houses. Each house had at least three to four garages. We drove a few blocks before pulled into one with red bricks, four car garage and a huge front yard with double doors. Hans pressed the garage button and pulled into one of the garages. He hopped out and opened the door for me. His garage was so neat. Each car had its own space. All the tools had a place on the magnetic wall.

"You love cars, huh?"

"Something like that." He closed the car door.

I watched as he grabbed my duffle bag out the back and then motioned for me to follow him into the house. He hit the lights, put the security code in and put my duffle bag on the large kitchen island. I sat down on one of the stools and he looked across at me. The house was a cool temperature, yet the way he stared at me made me warm.

"Want something to drink?"

"Yes," I watched as he pulled a glass bottle with water and poured some into a cup. He slid it across the counter while staring me right in the eyes. Why the hell was he making me feel like this? At the lounge, we kicked it and were having a great time and I didn't feel like that. Now, I felt like I was about to explode if he looked at me like he was one more time.

"I'm thinking we can go out to dinner tonight... I know you probably want to rest."

I shrugged. "Dinner sounds cool. Where am I sleeping?"

He grabbed my bag and touched my cheek before motioning me to follow him again. We walked upstairs and he went into a bedroom a couple doors down from the stairs. "This is the guest suite. Everything you need is in there. If you need something, let me know. My room is down the hall." He pointed to the room at the end of the hall.

"Is that where all the magic happens?" I flirted.

"Nah. My condo is where the magic happens. I told you I

don't bring bitches to my crib." He hugged me. "I'm 'bout to go in my office and finish some calls."

"Okay," I replied and watched him walk down the hall, then the steps. Closing the door, I leaned on the door and dialed Kenni's number.

When she didn't answer, I explored the room. It was a decent size room with a bathroom attached. The bathroom had one vanity, glass enclosed shower, and a garden tub. I could tell a woman had a hand in decorating his house. The décor was something only a woman would pick out. Still, it worked for his house and wasn't feminine. He didn't lie when he said I might want to rest. I tried Kenni's number again and when she didn't answer, I closed my eyes and got comfy under the covers.

Five

Hans

While Saylor was upstairs sleeping, I made a few calls, smoked another blunt and then settled on the back patio. It was breezy outside, but I did my best thinking out here. It didn't matter if it was snowing, I would push the snow off the patio set, sit down and get lost in my thoughts. Never in my life had I ever flew a chick in, and here Saylor was upstairs sleep in my guest bedroom. She was different. When she called me earlier I was surprised. I had been thinking about her since we separated that night. Each time I was about to call her, I decided against it. Women flocked to me, not the other way around. I had every woman out here wanting to be with me, or at least wanting to get hit with this dick. Relationships were something that I had never been into. I didn't trust people too easily, and women only wanted one thing; money. Even when I was broke I never had problems getting a chick. Women were a sucker for a nigga they thought was about to be next. Back home, bitches assumed that I was about to be next. I didn't know where they got that from, but I knew I wasn't about to be next. I carried myself differently from them niggas and they didn't like that shit. They didn't like me for doing me.

My only goals was for me and my brother to eat. I was all he had and he did his little hustling, but that wasn't enough. I had to pay the bills, feed us and buy that nigga clothes. Every time I turned around he was growing out of his shit. I never did this shit to floss on the next nigga. I hustled to survive. While niggas was taking their money getting fly or balling out on a whip, I was stacking money to the side and spending what I had to on what we needed. I was never worried about trying to look like I had money. In my opinion, there was a time and place for that. The same niggas that were buying jewelry, cars and spending money fast were the same niggas that lived in the next building or the floor below me. The moment I would stunt on these niggas would be when I had a crib out the hood and was making more than the bullshit I was being handed.

The hardest thing about leaving New York was leaving and not telling Saylor. I knew she would be fine because she was always fine. Saylor knew how to take care of herself. At the time, she was messing around with Darren so I knew if a relationship between the two didn't work, I knew that she would make sure he set her up so she could be straight. Saylor was different from other women. Even when she was just a teenager, she had a different thought process. While Kenni was floating around and trying to get with every drug dealer, Saylor wanted to be the drug dealer. Being a kept woman wasn't something that she was interested in. She wanted to be the one making her own money and never having to depend on a nigga. Even if I told her that I wanted her to come with me to

Virginia, I knew that she wouldn't come with me. Shit happened too fast and shit got real quick so we had to leave. There was no other option.

"We gotta get outta here now. Grab your shit and let's go," I told Haze who was dragging his feet.

I winched in pain at the bullet wound on my back. The hospital had advised me not to leave, but I had to go. I couldn't stay here another second. Especially knowing that my brother was out there while I was in the hospital. The nurse that worked on me gave me more pain killers than were allowed, extra bandages, and allowed me to discharge myself out the hospital.

"You're bleeding and shit. You should just go back to the hospital. I'm gonna be good while you heal up," he told me. I knew he was dragging his feet because he wanted to tell Kenni that he was leaving.

"Do you see what happened to me? That's not going to happen to you... they're going to fucking kill you, Haze!" I yelled and looked around.

This was supposed to be an in and out mission and he was making it longer than it needed to be. I had been planning on leaving for months before I told Haze the plan. The money and all the hours I spent hustling had been spent on setting shit up for us. New York wasn't for us and we couldn't make it here. If we continued here, we would look back and regret ever making the move. When our half-brother reached out, I was hesitant. He told me about our pops and how he wanted all of us to meet with him. That nigga could die for all I care. He left my mother and thought that he could rush back in and play the good parent. I held off on making any decisions, but still kept in contact with my half-brother. He was the one who told me about the money our father had and the business he had down in Virginia. Even then, I didn't give a damn and still continued to stack money here and keep my head low.

"I can't just leave, Kenni... I can't," he pleaded with me. Usually, I would give in to my brother and allow him to do what he wanted, even if it was something I didn't agree on.

"Kenni is laying with the nigga that ordered the hit on me... he wants me dead, and if you tell her, what the fuck you think is going to happen?"

"I already told her... A couple weeks ago when I saw her at India's party." He revealed and I slapped my hand across my head.

"Nigga, why the fuck would you tell her? You always following her around and you know the only shit she sees is money. How many times do I gotta tell you that?"

He looked down at his busted uptowns and then back to me. "Please, man."

"Who you more loyal to? Me or Kenni?" I hated to make him choose, but right now there wasn't no time for him to be stupid behind some pussy.

Kenni was cool people and we had known her mother, her, and her brothers for a while. I always looked out for her because she didn't have nobody to do that for her. When it came to Kenni and how she felt for Haze, I knew she didn't love him or care for him. To her, he was her raggedy next door neighbor that she hung out with when she was bored. Once they both hit eighteen, Kenni was worried about getting out the hood. And to her, the only way she was going to get out was by being a drug dealer's girlfriend. While Haze thought they were going to fall for each other, build and get out the hood while being together, Kenni was looking for anybody that had just a bit more money than Haze. He never wanted to admit it, but everybody saw that shit except him.

"You. And you know that shit. Why you even doing me like that?"

"Then prove that shit. Bridge is the nigga that wanted me dead and you bout to tell his girl where you're going. How stupid are you?" I hit him in the head and backed up. "I'm going to the car I bought, and if you're not down in ten minutes I'm out," I turned and left the door.

I maneuvered through the building and made it to the 91 Nissan Altima that I had bought from the chop shop. It was cheap and stable enough to make the journey to Richmond, Virginia. I made sure to get the windows tinted so that I could maneuver through the hood without anyone spotting me. According to everyone, I was dead. I had told him ten minutes but waited twenty. When the clock was nearing thirty minutes, I started the car and was about to take off when I saw Haze exit the building carrying a backpack and a small duffle bag. My brother meant a lot to me and I didn't want to leave him or put him in the position to choose. Still, my life meant something and I wasn't willing to die because he wanted to profess his love for a woman that would never listen to him.

"You better have a plan for Virginia. If we're moving to live the same way we're living here, let me know now." He turned and looked at me soon as he got into the car.

"Shit isn't going to be easy so I'm not promising you a free ride. All I'm promising is that in a couple years, we'll be glad that we left."

I guess that was good enough for him because he leaned back and put his seat belt on. We got on the highway and headed toward Staten Island. Before getting on the bridge, we stopped for some gas and snacks and headed into Jersey. Haze let his window down and chucked his phone off the bridge and into the water. He rolled the window up and leaned back in the chair as I drove.

"Why did Bridge try to get you killed?" he broke our silence.

"Because he heard I was talking to his supplier and thought I was trying to cut my own deal behind his back."

"Were you?"

"Nah. I'm loyal. Almost too loyal to the wrong people. His supplier wanted to talk to me because he believed that Bridge was fucking up in New York."

"And he got tight and tried to get you killed."

"Yeah."

What everyone thought was that Bridge was the supplier and made all the moves. It worked like that only in his head. The nigga had to answer to someone just like we had to answer to him. Julio was a small Columbian nigga with an even shorter temper. When he came into town, I happened to be with Bridge and was able to meet him. We met and somehow he had got my information and wanted me to meet with him – alone. I was weary at first. Julio was the type of nigga that you didn't tell no, so I ended up meeting him at this steak house in Long Island. We spoke and he told me he wanted me to run New York instead of Darren. He told me that Bridge had made a stupid mistake by letting his silly cousin take over prime real estate. I thought the meeting was a secret until Bridge pressed me about it. I was making my usual rounds and then I heard a gunshot and I was the nigga laying on the ground. My adrenaline was pumping too hard for me to lay there and die. I got up and ran six blocks to the hospital before I collapsed in the lobby of the hospital.

"You told me if I needed something to come and get you." Saylor was standing over me and I snapped from my thoughts from memory lane.

"Yeah, what you need?" I leaned up and put my blunt out and gave her my undivided attention. She had a towel wrapped around her body and her hair was pulled away from her face.

"You," she replied while staring me in the eyes.

A nigga was a little surprised when I heard what she said. "Me? Shorty I don't think you're ready for me."

"How about we let me decide what I'm ready for... okay?"

She turned and entered the house. I grabbed my phone and followed her into the kitchen. My dick was hard as shit and looking at her in that towel let me know she wanted me just as bad as I wanted her. That day when I put my hand in her panties and tasted her sweetness, I knew she had something that I couldn't rush right into. Saylor was a good girl and didn't give her kitty up to any and everybody, and I didn't want to take something that I knew I wasn't ready to deal with. She was digging into her purse and I snatched the towel off her body; exposing her naked body.

Saylor had the right amount of body for me. She was petite, nonetheless, she still had curves too. Her thighs, hips and ass was the perfect size for her body shape. Her breast had to be a B cup. Big enough for me to grip, and small enough to fit right in the palms of my hands without over-flowing.

"You snatched it off, what you going to do with it?" she turned and leaned on the counter.

I grabbed her little ass up and carried her into the dining room. Lowering her down onto my twelve seat dining table, I opened her legs and stuck my tongue right into her center. Since I had a taste all those years ago, her taste and scent had been something I had been looking for in other women. She tried to close her legs and I held them open while I snaked my tongue around her creamy center. She moaned out and put her hand on top of my head and guided me to where she wanted me to lick. I pushed her legs further apart, put them over my shoulders, and used my teeth to gnaw at her clit. Once she felt my teeth that's when her legs started shaking and she scratched my shoulders.

"Hans, you gotta stop," she panted.

"Why?" I said in-between slurps of her juices. "You really want me to stop?" I teased her and she nodded her head no.

Just when she was at her peak, I removed my tongue and pulled my jeans down and stepped out of them. I climbed on the table with her and got situated right between her legs. Pushing myself inside of her, the feeling of my member invading her insides sent chills down her spine. Her back arched and she looked me in the eyes with this lust filled look. I bit down on my bottom lip and pushed myself further inside of her while holding onto her hips.

"It's too big," she screamed out and tried to back away. I roughly pulled her closer, which made more of my dick enter her.

"You the boss, right? You can take this dick for me, right?" I asked and looked her straight in the eyes. Instead of speaking, she nodded her head and started to squeeze her pussy muscles on my dick.

I slowly pulled my dick out and pushed it back in a few times, then sped my pace up. I was kneeled on my knees and pulled Saylor up where she was just on me. I held onto her waist and slammed her down on my dick hard while biting on her neck. I heard screams, moans and pleads as I continued to do what I know best; fucking.

"I gotta cum again, ohhh, right there... fuck me, baby... fuck me!" she screamed out while she held onto my neck and bit down into my neck to muffle her moans. When her body got limp, I turned her over where she was on her knees and kissed her ass cheeks. She was so fucking beautiful that I wanted to kiss her everywhere. Time had only got better for Saylor.

"Aye, toot that ass up for me," I tapped my hard dick on her ass cheek. "Don't leave me with a hard dick," I told her. "And don't you nut until I tell you," I told her and pushed my dick right inside of her.

Her asshole quivered at the feeling of me going in from the back. I held her neck up and kissed her on the cheek while I fucked her from behind. Her hair was all sweated out and she was screaming and moaning again. I hit that shit so hard I was sure my table was about to break right under us. Digging my nails into her side, I pulled my dick out while holding her neck and shoved that shit right back into that warm, gushy pussy.

"Don't fucking nut until I tell you... ight?"

"Yes..." she moaned.

"Yes, what?"

"Yes daddy!" she screamed out and I smirked. Either time had softened her, or she hadn't had no dick like this in a long time. Either way, the sound of her calling me daddy made my dick harder.

We fucked on that table for another hour and my dick was still hard. "I gotta cum, daddy... can I cum?" she begged.

I never pictured Saylor being so submissive when it came to fucking, but shorty was submissive as fuck. "No, hold onto it for me, baby. Daddy about to unload soon," I promised her and held her ass up and shoved my dick right back inside. She was so wet that I had to keep pulling out and shoving my dick back inside to feel that gushy ass feeling. I slapped her ass hard and then pushed myself back inside. After a few strokes and hearing Saylor scream my name, I was about to cum. "Cum with daddy," I told her and felt her entire body become limp.

We stayed in the same position for twenty minutes trying

to catch our breaths before she broke our silence. "I can't believe that just happened."

"Shorty, that was years in the making. That needed to happen. We left it unfinished for years," I opened her legs and stuck my tongue right inside and she allowed me to continue to eat her pussy while she guided my head. When I felt her cream, I licked that shit up and gave her a kiss on her twat and looked at her.

"You're going to make me lose my mind, Hans," she said breathlessly. "What was that?" she leaned up.

"I like eating *your* pussy," I admitted. If you asked any chick I been with, I never ate pussy. Mainly because half these chicks wanted any nigga with money. I wasn't about to eat their pussy not knowing if they had the next nigga in that shit right before they came to see me. When I tasted Saylor's shit years ago, it was just a taste, but I knew that she had what I needed. When I opened her legs and tasted her an hour ago, the smell, the taste and everything surrounding that shit opened me up like a fucking window. I wanted to taste her again and again.

"You tell that to all your other chicks." She scooted off the table and stood and looked at me. "Don't gas me up. Please. I've had enough of that only to end up looking stupid." She walked back in the kitchen and I pulled my draws on and followed behind her.

"The fuck just happened?"

Saylor turned around with tears in her eyes. "I've never been fucked that way before. If I didn't know any better, I would say you fucked me with love, Hans. The way you took control, made sure I got mine off and then demanded my body...T...that's never happened to me before." She wrapped the towel around her body.

When I thought about it, I probably did fuck her with care and love. I wouldn't go as far as saying we made love, but I cared about if she was satisfied. I never gave a fuck about anybody else. I didn't care if they got off, long as my dick was emptied. With Saylor, I wanted her to be satisfied, I wanted her to scream my name and moan out for me during sex.

"Then why are you crying, Shorty?"

"Because once this is over I'll go back to New York and you'll go back to your life. I don't know...I'm super emotional right now," she wiped her tears and headed upstairs.

"Good dick will do that to you," I mumbled and went into my office to put in an order for my favorite seafood spot.

When I finished, Saylor was in the bathroom. I walked into the bathroom and she was in the shower washing her hair. I dropped my draws and got into the shower with her. When she felt my arms wrap around her, she melted. What had this woman been through? Had she never had a nigga hold her up? Soon as she felt my touch she melted into my arms. Even with her face being wet, her red eyes told me that she had still been crying. Had she been so used to carrying the world on her shoulders that she hadn't met that man that would partake in her burden of the world?

"Look at me," I held her chin and she looked me in the eyes. "I'm not going anywhere. I promise."

"I've been promised so many times," she admitted. "I've been hurt so many times. Hans, I don't want to hurt anymore."

I pulled her into my arms and hugged her while she sobbed. Saylor had always been my baby back in the day. I just knew I would always end up with her, or a woman just like her. Seeing that I had left her and she had to go through heartbreak after heartbreak to make her way to me hurt me. I pulled her away from my chest and stared her right in the eyes.

"Saylor, I put that on my life that I got you."

Even with her shaking her head, I knew I had to prove what I was saying to her. She had been hurt so many times that she needed some action behind the promise that I made her. After we showered, I towel dried her and applied lotion all over her body. The food arrived and I lit candles and ate with her over candle light.

"I'm sorry. I don't know what happened or what came over me," she apologized as she bit down into a shrimp.

"You don't need to apologize for feeling."

"I do. You know me, Hans. That's not me. I've always been satisfied after sex and ready to move onto the next thing. It was something about what we did that opened my emotions." She shook her head. "I don't know. It was different. All of this is different." She pointed at the candles and the seafood plated on the plates.

"I believe women that are worthy deserve to be treated like Queens and fucked like one. I only did what I saw. I saw a Queen and acted accordingly."

"I guess I'm just used to doing things different."

I laughed. "Shorty, what type of niggas have you been dealing with? I'm not the best nigga, but the women I've dealt with knew what it was when it came to me. You, on the other hand, you're not those women."

"Did you really mean what you said?"

"'Bout what?"

"Having me."

"Without a doubt."

"We haven't been in contact for years, Hans. You're willing to do all of this for me, and promise to have me and we just came back into each other's lives? I call bullshit."

I took a sip of my drink and sat it down. "I don't believe in coincidences. I believe everything happens for a reason. Kenni getting connected with Meeka again, being at the house when Haze rolled up. I believe all of that was supposed to happen. Whether it happened last week or next year, this was supposed to happen. When shit like this happens you're not supposed to take it lightly. That's the man in charge giving us a second chance or telling us what we're supposed to do. Back then, we weren't ready. We had a lot of shit going on where it couldn't work for either of us. I'm not willing to let a couple more years go past for this to line up again." She looked me in the eyes and I could tell she was wowed by my words.

She leaned on her hand and stared me in the eyes. "You believe that we were supposed to be together."

"Hell yeah. There's a reason relationships never worked out for me. There's a reason relationships never worked out for you. It sucks you had to get your heart broken, but that's the lesson in all situations."

"You're really speaking some real shit."

"Man, don't get me started about shit. I can go for hours talking about shit," I waved her off. I loved having deep and meaningful conversations. I wanted to know why people thought the way they did, or what people believed in and why? That shit was a turn on.

"Kenni hates when I get all deep," she smiled.

"Get deep with me. I wanna know everything and I wanna know why you feel a way. Me and Haze is always having this deep ass conversations with each other," I reached across the table and touched her hand. "When I say I got you... I really mean that shit. I'm not saying that we gotta get married, move in and all that shit right away. All I'm saying is that I'm not looking for nobody else and I hope you're not looking for nobody else."

She rubbed my thumb and smiled at me. "I'm not looking for nobody else."

Kenni

WHAM! Wham!

MY HEAD HIT the glass in Bridge's truck as he struck me for the third time. "I told you about making me look stupid in the store. I don't know that bitch and I told you that the baby not mine. Do that baby look like one of my kids?" he hollered so hard that spit flew from his mouth and hit the dashboard. "Always acting like a simple bitch whenever we get out," he continued.

We were shopping for a birthday gift for Ava, Supremes' wife. I had told Bridge that I could go alone, but since I got back from Virginia he followed me everywhere. I guess he was scared that I ran away the first time and thought I would do it again. While we were shopping, some chick rolled over with a new baby in the stroller. She kept trying to get Bridge's attention on the low and he hadn't noticed her. When we moved over to the purses, she followed over there and tried to act like she was looking for a bag too. Soon as I acted like I was going to use the bathroom; the bitch made a B-line over to Bridge and started hugging and talking to him. What pissed me off the most was that Bridge was over there talking and hugging her back. He even pulled the hood of the car seat back and kissed the baby. When I came back over, they both tried to act like

Bridge was asking her opinion on a bag for me. Bridge never shopped for me, he handed me the money. For my nineteenth birthday he went and shopped and got me clothes, sneakers and heels because he fucked up. After that, he never did that shit again.

I went off and mushed the girl in the head and cursed him out. Bridge loved to cheat and disrespect me in public but hated when I embarrassed his ass in public. He could do whatever he wanted and I was supposed to remain cool while he continued to fuck me over. He had got another chick pregnant and she had his baby. I was so stupid for coming back and dealing with him. I wanted to cry when I thought about all the shit I put up with when it came to Bridge. His hand problem never stopped, although he promised that he would. He was the same man and didn't come through on any of the promises that he had made to me in that hotel room. Who am I kidding? Did I really truly believe that he would change? When I got home he surprised me with flowers and a card with money to go shopping with. The sit down with India and Mercedes never happened. He had no plan on getting all three of us together. He knew his secrets would come out the closet and his ass would be caught. Messing with Bridge, one of those hoes were probably pregnant again and he was trying to avoid me finding out.

"I'm getting real sick of the same shit," I said while rubbing the temple of my head. "All you do is run around the city and fuck like a little ass boy."

Whap!

"Who the fuck you calling a little boy, Kenni? Since you been around that bitch Saylor you been acting real slick with the mouth. Next time I'm gonna knock those pretty ass teeth down your throat.

"You claim you love me, but you put your hands on me. What kind of love is that?" Tears flew down my cheeks.

My head felt like someone had dropped a rock on it, and I was tired of dealing with the same shit when it came to Bridge. I shouldn't have been surprised when it came to Bridge. There was probably so many women out there with kids that I didn't know about. He kept everyone out his business and the only person that knew was Supreme. Supreme was his best friend and would go to the grave with any secrets he held for Bridge.

"I love your stupid ass more than I love myself. Why the fuck you think I've put up with your shit all these years?"

If looks could kill, he would have flatlined behind the wheel of the car. "You put up with *my* shit? What exactly have I ever done during our relationship? I've done nothing but sit by your side and be a good woman for a no good man."

Whap!

This time he punched me in the side of the face. Whenever shit got real, he hated to hear the truth. He would rather put his hands on me than face the truth of his actions. I noticed he didn't take the exit to our home.

"Where are we going?"

"We're having dinner over at Supremes' crib. His wife's birthday is today and we're showing up without a fucking gift."

I rolled my eyes and leaned back in the chair. "Can we at least stop home so I can freshen up?"

"No," he said and turned the music up and tuned me out. As we drove, I looked out the window and silently cried. I cried because of my own stupid actions. I had my out and could have been free. Except, I felt bad and believed all the promises that I knew were lies.

We pulled into Supreme and Ava's driveway and Bridge killed the engine, got out, and walked toward the house.

I flipped the mirror down and fixed myself before getting out and walking behind him. Supreme didn't need me to say anything. He already knew that Bridge had knocked me around on the way here.

"Hey sis... Thanks for coming." He hugged me.

"You and I both know I didn't have a choice," I replied and entered the house. Ava was dressed in a silver sparkle dress with black Louboutin's. Her hair was pulled into a high pony. When she saw me, she ran over and hugged me.

When Supreme told us he was getting married both Bridge and I were a little confused. We didn't even know the nigga was dating anyone to get married. Supreme had always been low with his personal business. When I met Ava, she was perfect. She loved the hell out of Supreme and wasn't after his money. That was always a plus when it came to Bridge and Supreme.

"Hey, come with me to the bathroom," she whispered and whisked me off to the bathroom. She closed the door and grabbed a cotton swab. "Your nose is bleeding and the side of your face is already bruising. He did this on the way over here?"

Ava wasn't a stranger to Bridge's abusive ways. She realized two months into her marriage with Supreme that his best friend was a damn monster. "He got another damn baby," I sobbed and slapped my hands on my thigh. These days, I didn't give a damn who knew that I was abused. Maybe if these bitches knew the real Bridge maybe they wouldn't have been so pressed to take my spot.

"Are you really that shocked, Kenni," she pursed her lips and looked at me with one hand on her hip. "Bridge fucks with anybody and if I told you everything I heard; you would just brush it off as those girls are jealous. Yes, some of them are, but some of them aren't lying."

"I don't want to hear this," I sighed.

"You never want to hear it. Let me go and find some foundation so I can cover your bruises," she replied and quickly left out of the bathroom.

The door opened and Bridge slipped inside. "You know I hate this shit, right? You think I want to keep doing this?" he locked the door.

"Yet, you keep doing it to me. Do you think that I want to walk around with bruises on my face? Maurice that shit is embarrassing," I cried and he walked over to me.

He pulled me up from the toilet and sat me on his lap. "Ma, you make me crazy when you come at me with all that yelling. Especially when it's bitches that I don't even know. I don't know that bitch. Why you worried about her?" he kissed me on the lips.

"K." was all I could mutter because he was lying to me. Lying to me like he always did. Bridge didn't give a damn about anybody except himself. He didn't care about how I felt or how he made me look. I couldn't even go into Juleena's shop to get my hair done anymore. All they did was talk about Bridge and who he was seen with the night before, or claiming they have his baby.

"Look at me," I turned to look him in the eyes. "I love you."

"Me too."

"I saw on the app that you're ovulating," he held his phone up in his hand. "I wanna make my little girl," I could feel the bulge in his pants.

"Maurice, do you really think I'm in the mood?" He reached his hand around and stuck his hands in my leggings, then panties and felt my moist pussy. It was like my body and mind never agreed on anything. In my head, I was over it and didn't want to have sex with him. Then, he would touch my cat and that disloyal bitch would go ahead and get wet for him.

"Your pussy saying something different." He stood me up, pulled his pants down and stroked his dick a few times before pulling my leggings and panties down and sitting me right on his dick.

Bridge no doubt was blessed below. It was probably why he kept blessing other bitches. He held onto my hips and thrusted himself inside of me. "Bridge," I tried to speak, but it was feeling too good.

"Go ahead and ride daddy... do it like I like."

I held onto the sink and the tub and grinded my hips and bounced up and down on his hard dick. He held onto my hips and the door knob turned, but didn't open. "Kenni, are you good?"

"Yesssss," I moaned out because despite me not wanting any dick, it felt good. "I'm good, Avaaa," I moaned out.

"She good. Give us a minute," he called out and continued to fuck me. He picked me up and put me on the sink and then shoved his dick inside of me. "I love you. Ain't no nigga gonna love you like I do," he said with each thrust. "This pussy mine. I'm gonna do better," he said all the same shit whenever we fucked. That was the downside of our twisted relationship. We both enjoyed to fuck and we both knew how to fuck. No matter how angry, we would fuck until we couldn't anymore. Like now, I was upset with bruises on my face and here I was getting fucked on the sink in his best friend's house, at his wife's party. When I felt Bridge's hand tighten and him stiffen, I knew he had come.

"More, I didn't cum yet," I told him.

"Nah. Get cleaned up so we can start eating," he told me before kissing me on the lips, picking his pants up and leaving out the bathroom.

I hated that when Bridge came first he was quick to move on. He never let me get mine off, which resulted in me taking a bath and using the jet or the faucet to get off. Ava came back into the bathroom as I was pulling my leggings up.

"You both made up?"

"No."

"I couldn't tell from the moaning and the sink moving."

I laughed. "Bridge thinks sex solves everything."

Ava lifted her eyebrow. "Does he think that, or do you make everything better once sex is involved?"

She had a point. "Just fix me up, bitch," I joked.

"I'm gonna make you look like a damn clown if you keep it up."

After having dinner at Ava and Supremes' house, Bridge dropped me off at home and said he had to handle some business. I set the security alarm and went right to run me a bath. I put Sade on and got to work with my fingers down below. I pictured everything except Bridge's hateful ass. I had my legs spread apart as I let the faucet run full blast on my clit and moaned out. I screamed out so loud that my cellphone scared the hell out of me. I grabbed my phone and answered, although I didn't recognize the number.

"Hello?" I sounded out of breath. I was ready for round two and whoever this was, was interrupting my personal time.

"You still got that cute ass voice," I instantly recognized Haze's number. After I had to end our night and head to Juleena's side, we exchanged a few text messages and that was that. I got back to my life and I figured he did the same, so there was no need for me to reach out.

"Hey Haze... why isn't your number coming up?"

"I got a new number."

"Oh, so you can call me without Whitney going through your phone," I giggled into the phone.

"Whit knows who I'm talking to and what I'm doing. I'm a grown ass man."

"Let me speak to her. I wanna say hey, I miss her," I joked.

"Chill, you bugging." He laughed into the phone. "On the real, how you been? You been acting like a ghost and shit."

I'm good. I was just in the bubble bath."

"Probably popping your shit off, right?" I looked around.

"No."

He laughed loud as hell into the phone. "You were def finger fucking yourself. I could hear the shit in your voice."

"Haze, what the hell did you want?" I felt like the nigga had cameras around my house or something. How the hell did he know?

"Ight, ight. Saylor chilling out here and I thought you would be with her... come pop out... it ain't too long of a drive to Virginia."

"Saylor is not in Virginia," I protested.

"Hold on," he said.

"Hey Ken," Saylor got on the phone. "What you doing?"

"Saylor, how did you end up back in Virginia?"

"Me and Hans linked back up. I tried calling you, but you know how you never answer my calls," I felt bad because I did ignore Saylor's call when I was home. She either called when I was around Bridge, or when we spoke she was always trying to get me to leave. I didn't always want to hear that when I spoke to her.

"My bad. Y'all having fun?"

"We're about to head to the club... come out."

"I'm tired and had a long day," I lied. I wasn't tired, but I did have a long day of arguing and fighting with Bridge.

"Okay. Whatever."

"Damn, I thought Kenni was the party queen. I remember there was a time when you would party your ass off back in the hood." Haze came back on the line.

"We gotta grow up, you know? Y'all have fun at the party, okay?"

"Bet. Talk soon."

"Yep." We ended the call and the urge to masturbate had went away. I quickly rinsed off and got into the bed and watched the night news before dozing off.

"HEY BEAUTIFUL. I BROUGHT DONUTS," I walked into the kitchen where Juleena was sitting and eating breakfast with Brix.

She had surgery on her spine last week. Although she was back to feeling like normal, her leg was still in a cast and she had broken three fingers. She still needed help getting around and Brix was there for her through it all. From his eyes, I could tell that he was tired and needed a break, which is why I decided to come over today.

"You know I'm trying to lose weight. Not being able to move around has me already gaining weight," she pouted. "Am I fat, baby?"

"You already know you're not fat," Brix said and grabbed their dishes and put them in the sink. If I didn't know better, it seemed like he had a little attitude.

"Well, I guess I better toss these in the trash," I faked like I was about to toss the carton of donuts in the trash.

"Girl, don't be crazy. Give me a Boston cream right now," she clapped her hands together.

"Brix, go and get some sleep or go handle your business. I got her today," I smiled.

"Ight. Let me wash these dishes and I'm gone." He laughed.

"Don't be too glad to get rid of me," Juleena rolled her eyes.

I sat down and handed her a donut and ate mine. "I think I'm going to go to Virginia next weekend. Saylor is there and she's been having so much fun."

"Why is she up there?"

"We ran into some friends that we know from our old hood. Saylor been there since last week." Brix was a little too into our conversation, but I brushed it off as he hadn't had any decent conversation lately beside making sure the boys and Juleena were alright.

"Oh, okay. I was surprised she came up to the hospital with you when I got into the accident. She was acting real standoff like she didn't want to be there."

"Ju, you and Saylor haven't spoken in years. You both have this beef because Brix chose one and not the other. Do your really think she wanted to be there?" I asked with my eyebrow raised.

Juleena expected Saylor to just be cool with her because Brix decided to be with her. She felt like because she was the chosen one that Saylor was supposed to act like nothing happened and be friends with her because we were friends. I told Saylor a million times that she never had to be friends with Juleena because I was friends with her. And, Saylor never liked

Juleena. Since the first day they met, she told me she didn't like her and at first I thought Saylor was being shady, but I realized she had the right to pick and choose who she wanted to be friends with.

"I'm just saying. She's mad because she thought she and Brix had something. Clearly they didn't because look where he is." She rolled her eyes. "Brix better know I got eyes all over and if he's doing something wrong I'll know," she looked at Brix.

If I didn't know any better, it seemed like she knew something that neither me nor Brix knew. "Chill on talking about Saylor. We haven't been together in years." He put the last dish in the drainer and walked around the counter. "I got a couple runs to make. Thanks, Kenni," he said and headed upstairs.

"Things have been tense. Since I can't go upstairs I've been sleeping in the guest room alone." Juleena sighed.

"Alone? Why isn't he sleeping with you?"

"You know the guest room down here has a twin size bed. The two upstairs has the queen size beds. For the first few nights I was home, he slept on the floor, but now I feel like he wants some space away from me," she admitted.

"He's probably stressed."

Brix came back downstairs a couple minutes later and kissed Ju on the mouth before leaving out the door. "I feel like I'm putting all my time into the relationship and he's not. I really feel like I'm an inconvenience to him."

"Ju, you live in this man's home with your sons. You guys have been together for years now, and it's not all love and birds all the time. You guys have real bills and the boys to worry about. Then, this accident is something else. He's probably drained."

I had been around Juleena long enough to know that she was a brat. She loved having things her way and if they weren't, she threw a fit. Brix was a man that once stayed to himself and loved his space. He went from that to being home and caring for her. The man just washed the dishes and here she was complaining that she felt like an inconvenience. Juleena didn't realize how good she had it with Brix. Bridge's ass be ready to stomp my head off if I snorted the wrong way.

"I guess," I could tell there was so much she wanted to discuss, but she didn't feel like hearing me tell her that she was acting like a brat. "Anyway, there's not much for us to do. I can't really move like that." She sighed.

"We can go and sit in the living room and watch TV. I know there's something to watch." She waved me off.

"I'm tired of being in this damn house all the time. My doctor wants me on bedrest for another two weeks before I can go out." She complained.

"You're lucky to be alive and here for your boys," I reminded her. It was easy to complain about her condition now. It would have been a different story if we were burying her.

"I know and I sound crazy even complaining. I'm tired of being in the house all the time. Brix does his best to make me comfortable and I appreciate him for that. But, I miss getting dick. I feel like I have to beg him to get some dick."

"You have a spinal injury and your entire leg is in a cast. I agree with him not fucking you," I reminded her.

"Before all of this. I'm not in the mood lately, but I do miss feeling him inside of me. Before the accident, I felt like I had to beg him to have sex with me. Even when he did, it wasn't the same."

I came over here to get over my sad ass life and all she was doing was bringing me down. Juleena wasn't telling me something, and I didn't care to find out. Brix chose her, and that wasn't enough for her. She had to go ahead and throw Saylor's name up in fights between them. Even though she got Brix, Saylor was truly the one who won.

I gotta run to Miami for a couple days. Hold down the crib. Love u. Bridge sent me a text message and I rolled my eyes. He thought I was really dumb. Mercedes had been talking about a trip to Miami for the past month on her social media. The only reason I had her was because I refused for those bitches to have my number. We communicated via Facebook. When they needed to tell me something about the kids, or I had to pick the kids up I would shoot them a quick message. Mercedes had been going on and on about this trip and how she couldn't wait to take Mia to the beach and show her baby the world. I desperately wanted to comment on her post that taking your baby to Miami wasn't showing them the world. However, I played nice and worried about myself. What bothered me the most about Bridge was how he would get on my case when I came out my mouth to his baby mamas. But, when they said slick shit or did shit to me he never had time to put up with what he called petty bullshit.

I want to come. I'll be home soon.

Nah. It's not that kind of trip. I told you that already. C u when I get back.

Tell Mercedes and Mia I said hey. Fucking liar.

Yo, where you at? Every time a woman got crazy out the mouth, the first thing a nigga thought to ask was where they were. He didn't need to worry about where I was at. I planned to sit with Juleena until Brix got back, then I was going home to pack and head to Virginia. Since Bridge wanted to go have fun, I was about to do the same.

I'm going to drive in tonight. I'm gonna book my hotel. I sent

Saylor a quick message. We both needed to talk about why she was spending so much time there.

Ok. Text me when you leave and drive safe.

Alright.

I put my phone away and looked at Juleena who was feverishly texting away on her phone. She had this scowl on her face and I could tell whatever that was going on her phone screen wasn't good.

"Girl, what are you in a text battle?" I joked.

"Mama just sent me a text talking about she's going to pick the boys up, then come to spend the weekend at the house. Brix called her and told her that he had to go to Miami with Bridge."

"Bridge just told me he was going to Miami too."

She looked over at me. "Really? So maybe he's not lying to me."

With how insecure and paranoid Juleena was being, I wasn't about to tell her that Bridge was going to be with Mercedes and their daughter. All she would do is assume that Brix was going down there to cheat on her, and he could actually be going to do work while Bridge was going to fuck around.

"I know it's been tough, but he has to work. How do you think he's going to keep up living like this," I pointed around the house. "He has to work."

"You're right. I'm going to tell him sorry and to try and enjoy himself," she replied and got back to texting.

I sat with Juleena for another three hours before Brix came in with groceries. I knew she was itching for me to leave so she could ask him twenty-one questions, so I got my stuff and told her I would come stop by next week. Soon as I pulled into the driveway, I cursed myself for not staying away longer. Bridge's truck was parked in the driveway along with Supremes' car. I killed the engine and walked slowly to the front door. Soon as I stepped in, I heard Bridge laughing at something with Supreme. I followed his voice into the kitchen where they both were sharing a drink.

"Where you been all day?" he walked over to me and pulled my head back and kissed me on the mouth. "That little slick shit with the text message need to quit," he told me and released me.

"Let me get out of here so I could go pick Ava up. Last I heard from her she was in the mall picking up last minute shit." Supreme hugged me, then headed out the door.

There was no use in having an argument with him about going to Miami. It was clear he had everything planned out and that didn't include me. I sat my purse on the counter and headed upstairs. I wasn't stupid. My ass wasn't going to pack and leave until the morning. If Bridge even suspected that I was trying to leave he would put the plans for Miami on hold without a doubt.

"You don't have nothing to say?" he followed me into our bedroom. I went into the bathroom and took off my jewelry.

"What do you want me to say? You're going to go if I approve or not, so why even waste my breath?" I pulled my hair down from the bun and walked past him back into the bedroom.

Bridge fed off fights and getting a rise out of me. He loved when we argued so he could put my head through the wall. He was going to Miami and I wasn't making a big deal of it, so that was a problem. He wanted me to care and I didn't. When it came to Bridge, I was so done with giving a fuck. Each time I cared, he showed me why I shouldn't give a fuck. At this point, he and his little family he had with Mercedes could be together and I wouldn't give a fuck. All I craved was to be happy and not wake up every morning feeling like a boulder was sitting on my chest.

All I wanted was to laugh and smile again. It seemed like it had been a while since I've done either of those things. All I did was argue, cry and nurse the wounds given to me by the man that was supposed to love me. Bridge wanted to be able to do whatever he wanted and didn't want to answer to me. All I was, was his pretty trophy, his untouched fruit. All his niggas would give their last limb to be with me, and he loved that. He loved that he had a woman that men craved to be with yet couldn't be with.

"Why you always gotta start some shit before I leave?"

"Maurice, I'm damned if I do, and damned if I don't. Have fun in Miami and definitely be careful since you'll be handling business. I heard a rumor about you and Mercedes and shouldn't have believed it," I lied.

Bridge didn't do social media and both his baby mamas knew this. It was the reason they both ran to social media whenever something happened. Let him be late paying them one month and they would air his ass out like he was the worst deadbeat in the world. I mean, he was, still, he did a lot for those broke bitches. Social media should have been the last place they ran to air his business.

"See, this is the woman that I wanna wife. I'm tired of arguing about rumors when you know I love you. Look at this house, look at your closet and the two whips you got in the garage. All them bitches spreading rumors want all that you have." He looked at his ringing cell.

"And the bumps and bruises too," I mumbled while he picked up his phone. He quickly left the room so I couldn't hear what he was talking about. At this point, I didn't need to know who he was talking about. I knew he was probably talking to Mercedes and wanted me to believe he was handling business.

"Ight. I gotta head to the airport, baby...I'll be back in a few days. You gonna miss daddy?"

"You know I am. Be careful, okay?" I kissed him on the lips and hugged him tightly. I knew he thought everything was good with us, and it was. He was going to get out and have his fun, and I was about to go have my fun too. As much as he thought he was slick, I was already three steps ahead of his dumb ass. I played the stupid girlfriend and walked him to the door. I watched as he got in his truck and pulled out the drive way. I blew kisses and waved until I couldn't see his car no more. I locked the door and went upstairs to grab some things and pack for Virginia. I sent Saylor a message and told her I would arrive in the morning. Tonight was my night to sit back and enjoy having the house to myself before getting on the road in the morning.

Six

Brix

Me and Juleena sat in the living room while the boys played in their rooms. A few times I had to get up and play ref because they wanted to fight about toys that they both had. Juleena spoiled them to no end so they felt like they could do whatever they wanted. While she sat on the couch eating her Cheetos, she allowed them to scream, yell and curse to each other like it didn't bother her. I pulled the blanket over my legs and closed my eyes for a quick second to get some sleep. Miami was supposed to be on the agenda, however, Juleena threw a fit about me leaving her and the boys. Bridge had planned for Mercedes and their daughter to come down. He was on some pleasure shit, but I was there for business. We had a meeting with some Haitians down there and that was my main reason for going. It was also going to be nice to be out and chill alone. I didn't know the last time I had time for myself. My man cave in the basement had went from my personal space to a play-room for the boys. Ju argued that the boys needed a place besides their rooms to play. Me, trying to be a good man and step-father, I allowed her to turn it into the boy's playroom. I picked my house because I loved everything about it. Now, I wasn't too certain why I fell in love with it. Everything in the house screamed Juleena or the boys. I was tired of feeling like I was living in someone else's house. The shit was like a damn nightmare that I continued to relive all over every morning.

"Why you falling asleep? You always do that when we're watching a movie together," Juleena whined.

"Baby, I'm tired as shit. I been up since this morning running the boys around and then making sure they didn't beat each other up. A nigga need some sleep."

"What do you think is going to happen when we have a baby? You lose sleep when you have children, Brix."

"And all I'm saying is that I need some sleep. I'm not complaining."

"If you were in Miami you wouldn't be trying to sleep."

I sucked my teeth and pulled the cover over my head and closed my eyes again. My mind went straight to Saylor. I really fucked up when I picked Juleena over Saylor. I should have gone with my heart. Saylor had me fucked up because I knew a life with her was risky. She wasn't the type to sit at home and make a home. She wanted to be out in the streets right with me. It was the reason I decided to go. Everything about Saylor scared the shit out of me and I wasn't man enough to handle that. I feared that I would hurt her and break her heart. When I sat and thought about her, we were both scared and didn't know what we wanted. We didn't know how to start some-thing. What we had was so intense that neither of us knew how to deal with it. Juleena was safe. She was the woman that would make my house a home and not ask too many questions. She had prepared her entire life to please a man, and after getting a baby daddy that did nothing for their kids, she could appreciate a good man. She was the safe choice for me. Still, the safe choice wasn't the right choice. It was hard to say that I never was in love with Juleena. Especially because she was so in love with me. She was so in love with me and would do anything for me. On the other hand, I didn't feel the same about her.

"I'm going to go grab dinner from the chicken spot. What do you want?" I tossed the cover off my body and went to grab my sneakers.

Since Juleena was out of commission we had been eating out a lot. The boys had to eat and she did to, and I wasn't about to go in the kitchen and play chef with all that I had going on right now. So, instead of letting them starve, I had been going to get food from our favorite places. Shit that was similar to the stuff that Juleena would cook at home. The first week I spoiled the boys with McDonalds and all that other fast food shit. Jessica cooked a few times, but with her going through her own stuff I didn't expect her to cook for us. I was a grown ass man and could find a way to feed Juleena and the boys without her.

"I want a breast this time. They gave me a thigh and you know I hate the thighs," Juleena told me. "Oh and make sure to get extra biscuits," she added.

"Got you," I kissed her on the lips and grabbed my coat. The boys ran down soon as they heard my keys in my jacket.

"Where you going, Pops?" Julian, the oldest of the two asked.

"Going to grab some dinner."

"Can we have Wendy's? I don't want no more food from the chicken shack," Julius, the younger one asked.

"Nah, we need to eat shit that's close to mama's cooking. We can't be eating all that unhealthy shit," I told them.

"Ma, can I get Wendy's?" Julius went around what I said and asked his mother, knowing she was going to let him do whatever he wanted.

"Babe, just get them what they want."

"No. I said what we're getting and that's final," I hated when Juleena did that shit right in front of them. She wanted me to discipline and teach them how to be men, yet she was always undermining me and letting them do whatever they wanted.

"Wendy's. I want a spicy chicken," Julius told me.

"I said what I said. I'm not buying that shit."

"Aye, don't curse at my babies," Juleena jumped back in the conversation. "Let them get what they want, baby... hurry back."

I left out the house without saying another word. What was the purpose of arguing with her or them? She let them do whatever they wanted. Just last week they spent hella money on their x-box on her credit card and she punished them for one day. When I came home the next night they were up and on that game like nothing happened. I was so tired of her wanting me to be a part, yet she wanted to have the last say on things. It was the reason the sweet boys I met three and a half years ago were now little bastards who felt entitled. Even Jessica stopped coming around because they don't even respect their grand-mother. She believes they need their ass beat and Juleena disagrees and forbids anyone from doing it. I dialed Saylor's number. I had been hitting her since I found out that she was close. Part of me wanted to take the ride to Virginia to see if I ran into her. She had told me the hotel she was staying at the last time she was down here, so I wondered if she was staying there again.

"Hello?"

"What's up, Saylor? I been hitting you up, your phone fucked up or something?" I pulled out the driveway and sped out of our subdivision.

"No, I was ignoring your calls," she admitted. That was the one thing I loved about Saylor. She always told it like it was and wasn't afraid to speak her mind.

"Damn. What I do to deserve that?"

"Nothing, I just don't feel like getting involved in some shit that I'm going to end up being hurt in. You're with Juleena and that woman isn't letting you go," she replied.

"I plan on leaving soon, Say. I don't need you to believe me, but me and Juleena grew apart."

"Apart?" she laughed. "You never loved Juleena and forced that whole relationship. Brix, you don't have to lie to me. Where's the baby, ring, and all the bullshit? You both are the same place you were when you made your decision."

"Damn," I sighed into the phone. What more could I say? Everything she was saying was right. I didn't want to marry Juleena, although she always tossed out hints on the regular. She wanted to have a baby and each time that the month rolled by, I prayed that the pregnancy test would come back negative. I wasn't ready to have no kids with Juleena, especially the way she raised her kids. I noticed that early on and realized that I couldn't have kids with her. Shit, we couldn't even co-parent.

Her voice softened. "Brix, I'm not saying this to hurt your feelings... you know that," she whispered into the phone. "I care about you and never stopped. It's just that... I can't sit back and allow you to hurt me for the second time. I have to protect my heart."

All Saylor was doing was trying to protect her heart. She didn't want me to stomp on it the way I had years ago. It made sense why she was so guarded and closed off. She didn't want to end up fucked over in the end, and that was understandable.

"I hear you... How could my feelings be hurt by you spitting real shit to me? I want to see you."

"Bri—"

"I already know you in Virginia. I want to see you, Saylor," I cut her off. All that talk about trying to protect her heart was cool and I understood what she was saying. However, I wanted to lay eyes on her and feel her near me.

"I'm staying with someone so I can't invite you here."

"I'm gonna get a hotel room. When I text you the address and room number, I expect to see you there," I told her and ended the call.

Soon as I pulled in front of the chicken spot, my phone started to ring. Jessica's number popped on the screen. I answered thinking something was wrong. I mean, I had just left the crib and the chicken spot was about twenty minutes from our house.

"Hey Mama Jess, what's going on?"

"Why is Juleena crying about you cursing the kids out and leaving without saying anything?" I huffed into the phone. "Should have known her spoiled butt was being dramatic."

I loved Jessica because she saw right through the shit her daughter did, and she was quick to call her out when she needed to. "The boys want fast-food and I told them that they were getting whatever I bring into the house. Juleena is always giving them their way... I'm not gonna do that shit," I walked into the chicken spot.

My nigga that owned it already knew why I was there and nodded to let me know he was going to prep my order and bring it to my whip when it was done. "I told her years ago she needed to start whipping the boys. She thought because she put them in private school and all those fancy programs that it would work. Nothing works like a good old fashion ass whopping."

"I agree. Since I'm not their biological father I'm not going to put my hands on them. That doesn't mean that I'm not going to discipline and try and lead them to the right place."

"Juleena will get over it. I told her I would call you and find out what happened. She's miserable because she's in that cast and has to stay in that chair all day. Soon as she's healed up it will go back to normal."

"I hope so," I muttered.

What was really normal? The injuries were only the tip of the iceberg. Me and Ju had problems way before the accident. What made me curious was the fact that she was in Virginia the same time that I was. I wasn't buying that supplier meeting because she would have told me about that that morning. When I asked what she was doing, she said she had some appointments and was going to try and make it out the shop before the boy's recital. She never mentioned that she was going to be in Virginia. If she was going that far from the kids she would have let me know right away. The owner gently knocked on my window and broke me from my thoughts.

"Good looking, man. Here's some bread," I peeled off two hundred dollars. Keeping black businesses like this around was important. The meal cost no more than thirty dollars, but because he always went above and beyond when I came through, I wanted to pay him back for that.

"Your money is no good here, Brix. You're the reason I have so much business. Everybody comes in here because of your word of mouth. We appreciate you."

"I just tell them what I experience. Y'all good people. I'll be by tomorrow. I think we'll try the ribs."

"I'll have it ready for when you pull up." He dapped me through the window and went back into the restaurant. I pulled off back toward the house. Later when Juleena was asleep, I was going to book the hotel and tell her some bullshit excuse about having to handle some shit here because Bridge was gone. Juleena wasn't going to call Bridge and confirm because she wanted her cousin to believe she had the perfect life. Me and Bridge weren't as close as we used to be. I couldn't get down with how he treated Kenni. Unlike Saylor, I wasn't about to turn down bread for a woman that continue to come back to the abuse.

Juleena was pissed that I had to leave for a few days and she made sure to let me know. Jessica told me she would come and stay with her and the kids so that I didn't worry too much. I did worry about them when I was away, but at the same time I needed to get the hell away. I needed some time alone to do me and not feel guilty about it. Since me and Ju got together I never had time for me anymore. I wasn't a nigga that hung out every weekend, yet, if I wanted to chill with the niggas at the club on a Friday night, I did that shit. I did it without having to convince someone that I wasn't out paying attention to other bitches. Although my reasonings for getting away were dishonest, I was excited to lay eyes on Saylor. She was supposed to head back home but promised me she would kick it with me for a few days before going back home.

I checked into my room and looked at the view of the city from my room. Plopping on the bed, I laid back and stared out the window. Virginia was always one of my favorite cities to come to. I used to fuck around with a shorty that lived out here. Plus, I made hella money out this way. Bridge decided the money out here wasn't worth it and was focused on expanding away from Maryland. Since New York had been taken over since Darren's dumb ass got locked up, he had been putting all his efforts into expanding in Florida and California. None of what he was doing made sense and I made sure to tell his hard-headed ass this. He was the type that always did what he wanted and listened to himself, so I fell back and paid attention to what I needed to listen to.

Soon as I leaned back on the bed, Juleena's name popped across my screen. I just knew that she was going to call me. She had called me the entire ride up here and expressed how her mother didn't do this or that like I did, and how she was so miserable. She told me this shit like I didn't know that she was miserable. I mean, she told me about the shit every ten damn minutes when I was home. I answered the phone and put it to my ear.

"What's good, Ju?"

She was sobbing into the phone. "I miss you, baby. When are you coming home?" she continued to sob into the phone.

When I met Juleena, she was the strong ass boss woman that handled her shit. The way she raised her kids, handled her shops, and lived was a turn on to me. Just because I was never in love with her didn't mean that it wasn't a turn on to see an independent woman doing her thing. Now, all she did was cry, nag, and complain. She leaned on me for every damn thing. What happened to that boss chick that I first met? Where the fuck did she go?

"Stop crying, Ju. I'm not even going to be gone that long.

Your moms wiped your shitty ass when you were born, I'm sure she got you now."

She sniffled and giggled through her tears. "I know. I just miss you and want to lay up under you. You're my favorite person."

"You're my favorite person too. Stop giving your moms a hard time. She's doing her best... you hear me?"

"Yeah, I hear you."

"Make sure the boys are listening too. If I find out they been misbehaving, I'm taking the Xbox out of their rooms," I sternly told her.

"Okay," I knew she was half listening. When it came to disciplining the boys she always tuned me out. This time, she wasn't about to do that shit to me. I was going to punish they ass if they were misbehaving with their grandmother.

"Talk to you later. Try and get some rest."

"I am trying. I just miss our bed and lying beside you. It makes me sad; you know." She sighed.

"Yeah, I miss you up there," I missed waking up to my hard dick in Juleena's mouth. Since we moved in together I woke up every morning to head. Even when she was sick, she was still down there slobbing on my knob. It was something that I could admit that I had become spoiled with.

"I know you miss me shoving that dick down my throat." My dick grew hard at the mention of her giving me head.

"I'm 'bout to come down there and drop it in your mouth," I joked.

"Please," she pleaded. "Baby, I miss tasting you."

"Ma, I'm not worried about head. I'm worried about you getting back right. There will be a time for that. Right now, we need to worry about you."

"Okay. Talk to you later."

"Okay," I ended the call and tossed it near the pillows on the bed.

After taking a shower, I ordered room service and was sitting in the seating area catching up on the game and eating the pizza I had delivered to the room. The tap at the door caused me to put the pizza down and open the door. Saylor was standing there dressed in a pair of sweats, crop sweater and her hair was braided into two braids. She was dressed down and still looked better than these bitches that put all that makeup and shit on.

"You look good," I complimented and pulled her into a hug. We hugged for a minute before she broke our embrace. "Smell good too."

"Thanks. You too," she walked in and put her purse on the table and looked around the room. "How was the drive?"

"Good. I did a lot of thinking so it seemed shorter than usual." On the drive up, I had thought about so much shit that by the time I pulled up to the hotel my head was about to spin.

I thought about my relationship with Juleena, my situation with Saylor, and what I truly wanted. I couldn't think of Saylor or Juleena, I had to put myself first and what I wanted. Did I want to try and make it work with Juleena? We had so much history. We had a home we created together. Did I want to give that all up? Or did I want to work on shit and communicate the shit that I didn't like. I had all these complaints, but never voiced them to Juleena. Knowing her, she would be willing to work on things and try to change them. Then I thought about Saylor, she was who my heart desired and I always thought about what if I decided to be with her. Where would we be? Would she have moved to Maryland for me? Would we share a home together? Have kids and a relationship people dreamed of? Or would we have been playing the same two step we've always played?

The intense game of who wants to open up first? Would I still be working double time breaking down the walls she had built up around her heart? Trying to get her to see that I loved her and that I would never intentionally hurt her. It was hard to picture it because years had passed and she was still the same woman. She wasn't that same eighteen year old who was dying to be introduced to the drug game, but she had no kids, no serious relationship, and I could tell she was still guarded. I knew from Kenni that she didn't date. It often made me wonder if I made the right decision? Although there was chemistry with me and Saylor, was it meant for us to be together? Were we the perfect match? Or were we both gluttons for hurt feelings? It was an even exchange; she provided the heart and I provided the hurt.

"Hello?" Saylor waved her hand in front of my face. "You just zoned out like you were Raven from Disney," she laughed.

"My bad. I been having a lot on my plate and tend to do that shit often."

"How is Juleena? She good?"

"She's getting better. I'm surprised that you asked about her."

Saylor sat down on the couch and took a slice of pizza. "I don't want the woman dead. She has two kids and her accident was serious."

"Yeah. It was." The room grew quiet and neither of us said anything. The TV was background noise. I sat down beside her and leaned back. "I missed you."

Saylor looked me in the eyes before her gaze dropped to her hands. "I've missed you too."

"Why we keep fighting this shit?"

Saylor sighed. "We both know that we can't be together. You forgot that we walked down that road before. You have a home with Juleena. I can't be responsible for breaking that up."

"What if you're not responsible for breaking that up?"

"Before we ran into each other in Maryland, were you thinking about ending things?"

I grew quiet.

"Exactly. You weren't thinking about ending the relationship. Did you think about the regrets you have, sure. However, you weren't worried about ending things with her."

I pulled her onto my lap and to my surprise she didn't protest. I turned her face to mine and kissed her on the lips. She allowed me to take control and kiss her on the lips.

"Doesn't matter if I was thinking about it or not. It's always been you and we've both fought it. I may have chosen Juleena, but you let me choose her."

"You're going to really blame your decisions on me?"

"Say, you didn't fight. You didn't show me that what we had was what you wanted. You made it seem like it was nothing to you. I had a chick ready to do any and everything, and then one who brushed shit off. I may have made the decision, but you helped make that shit easier."

She held my face and kissed me on the lips. The only thing that could be heard through the apartment was the sound of our lips kissing and the highlights from the game on the TV. I pulled away and then sucked on her bottom lip once more. I wanted her. And, I wanted her in the worst way possible. If life was easy, I could end things with Juleena, and start my life with Saylor. Even if I was to completely walk away from Juleena, I couldn't jump right in with Saylor. Being with Saylor was like trying to master the tango. You had to move the right ways and make the right moves to enter her heart. Not just anybody got the pleasure of holding her heart, and she made sure of that shit.

"I don't know if I should be doing this," she hopped off my lap and stood in the corner. "I'm kind of with someone."

"He must not mean shit if you right here with me. I didn't force you here, you came willingly."

"I'm not blaming you on how I got here. All I know is that I have something going on and I care for him. I really do," she admitted, as tears fell down her cheeks.

"He means more to you than I do?"

"I knew him before I knew you. That's not fair, Brix. I never asked you that question or put you in the position to answer that question."

"Answer the question."

She grabbed her purse and headed to the door. "I can't do this right now," she said and jetted out the door.

I followed behind her into the hallway. "Saylor!" She stopped but didn't turn around. "You know I fucking love you. I've made mistakes in my past and hurt you, but I didn't mean to hurt you. I want to make it right and be with you."

"How? How can you be with me when you have Juleena? As bad as I want to go into the hotel room and make love to you, I know that's only setting me up to hurt myself again." She pressed the elevator and waited without turning to look at me. "I deserve to be happy, Brix. Not just you," she said and stepped on the elevator when the doors opened.

I leaned on the wall and put my head in my hands. To have her in my arms and then to slip right out killed me to my core. However, I heard everything that she said.

Seven

Bridge

I TRIED Kenni's number again from the hotel phone and it went to voicemail. Her ass didn't go nowhere, so why the hell was her phone going to voicemail. I put the phone back down on the receiver and sat on the edge of the bed. Last night when I spoke to her she sounded like she was out. The only friend she had in Maryland was Juleena, and her ass wasn't going to be out and about for some time. I scratched my beard and leaned back on the bed.

"She didn't answer again," Mercedes asked and rubbed my chest. "You think she's out there cheating on you?"

"Kenni not stupid. She's a good girl... she don't let no other dick up in my pussy." Mercedes rolled her eyes and leaned her head on my chest.

Mercedes used to be good like Kenni, but she let her ratchet ass friends pump her head up. After we lost our first baby, she let her friends fill her head up. She fucked one of my niggas. After I beat that nigga into the concrete, I looked at Mercedes like she was soiled. It was because she was soiled. I could never wife a bitch that let another fuck while being with me. She thought because I was out there doing my dirt that I was going to forgive her. It didn't work like that. When you were with me, you had to be clean and untouched. I wanted a bitch that every nigga wanted, but never had the pleasure of touching. I heard Kenni had got around in her hood. Niggas didn't speak on that shit, and I hadn't met the nigga who had fucked her, so she was clean to me. Since I been hitting that pussy she hadn't had no other nigga in that shit, so she was pure to me. Mercedes let too many niggas hit her shit and thought that I would wife her. I could never be with her like we used to be again. This little trip was because she was hell bent on making memories for Mia's baby books. I agreed with her though. My daughter deserved to have pictures of both her parents being happy.

We got a suite at the four seasons and I had been fucking Mercedes in every hole since we arrived. Mercedes had no problem pleasing me whenever I wanted. She thought by each suck or nut that she was securing her position. It was the reason she kept trying to plant that Kenni was cheating in my head. Kenni knew better and I didn't have to worry about that when it came to cheating on me. If she knew what was good for her, she would sit her ass down and wait for me to return home.

"Can we stay a few extra days? I'm not ready to go back home." Since I handled the meeting I had down here, I was ready to head back home.

"I don't know, Mercedes."

She pulled the covers back and pulled my dick out. "How about now?"

"I still don't know. I been down here three days already."

She licked the shaft of my dick and looked me in the eyes. "I want to spend more time with you and Mia." She kissed the tip of my dick before shoving it down her throat. A nigga damn near arched his back when I felt her tonsils. Mercedes was second runner up when it came to Kenni. She knew how to suck a nigga' dick clean off his body. She was just about to choke on my shit when Mia started crying from her room. Mercedes hopped right up and went to tend to our daughter. India and Mercedes were night and day. Mercedes didn't play when it came to Mia. She handled everything about our daughter and made sure she was always good. Even when it came to her going out and having her time, she made sure our daughter was taken care of. My daughter never smelled like spoiled milk and she was always dressed in the newest shit.

She came strolling back into the room twenty minutes later. "She was hungry so I got her some cereal and put her favorite show on. I know when I go back out there she's going to be asleep. She's not done sleeping, but she too nosey."

"Daddy's girl always has to know what's going on," I laughed.

"She really believes she runs the house," Mercedes sat down on the bed. "I wanted to talk to you about something."

"Oh yeah? What's that?"

"I want to have another baby. I'm ready to try for baby number two." She rubbed my thigh and looked me in the eyes. "Mia is three and she keeps asking about a baby brother. I want to at least give her a sibling and I want them to have the same parents," she further explained.

"Me and Kenni trying to get pregnant right now, Cedes. I

can't give you another baby before giving her one. She might just leave me this time."

"I'll tell everyone it's by someone else. I won't say it's by you... please baby," she pulled my dick back out and started sucking on just the tip. She knew I loved that shit. It was like she sucking on a lollipop. The sound she made did something to me too.

"Ight. You better keep this shit quiet because Kenni's not going to go for another baby. She already tried to leave."

Mercedes pulled her pajama bottoms off and slid down right on my dick. I filled her up and she started bouncing on my shit while I spread her ass cheeks apart and matched her speed. I loved my kids and Mercedes was a good ass mother and deserved to have another kid. If I could give India's dumb ass two seeds, I could give Mercedes the same. My main focus was on giving Kenni one of my seeds. I even made her sync her ovulation and period app to my phone. She never reminded me when she was ovulating. I always got the alert and didn't give a damn where I was at. I'd pull this dick out and fuck the shit out of her and make sure I nutted all into her. Shooting my seeds up into pussy wasn't the problem. Shit, when I looked at bitches I could get them pregnant. I think those miscarriages did something to her body because she should have been pregnant by now. The hotel's phone rang and I grabbed it while Mercedes was riding the shit out of me.

"Hey. My phone was in the bedroom. I was taking a shower," Kenni's voice came through the line. Mercedes had no problem getting my dick hard. When I heard Kenni's voice, it made my dick ten times harder. "How's Miami?"

"What that got to do with it going to voicemail?"

"Bridge, I don't know. Could be the service in the house or

something. Didn't I call you back?" she huffed into the phone. That attitude was what got her ass slapped around.

"Ight. Where you at?"

"I just told you. I'm at the house, Bridge," she snapped.

"Yo, watch your fucking mouth and that attitude," I barked, while Mercedes did the reverse cow girl. She bounced that shit up and down so hard that I damn near moaned into the phone.

"Baby, uhh," Mercedes moaned and I covered the mouth piece of the phone.

"What was that?" Kenni questioned.

"I'm on the balcony. The hotel only had rooms near the damn pool... loud ass people," I lied my ass off.

"Oh. What's up?" Something was different in her voice. I couldn't put my finger on it, but there was something different with the way that she was talking.

"Fuck you mean, what's up? What you been doing?"

"The same thing I do when you're home; nothing."

"Shitttt!" I couldn't help but to yell that out because Mercedes was working hard for that baby. "Dropped my damn blunt."

"That sounded like a fucking moan! Are you fucking somebody, Maurice?" she yelled. "Please tell me that you're not fucking some bitch while you're on the phone with me." It was like she was daring me or some shit.

"Kenni, you sound stupid as fuck. Why the fuck would I be fucking a bitch while on the phone with you? I called to check on you, but you must be on your period with the way you spazzing."

"When are you getting back?"

"Why?"

"Because I want to know. I was going to hang with Saylor

and wanted to know when you were coming home," I heard someone in the background talking and leaned up. "Hello?"

"Who the fuck was that?"

"S...Saylor," she stammered. "She came to keep me company." The shit that I hated about Kenni was that I could never tell if she was lying or not. She was so good at covering up a lie that I never knew when her ass was lying to me.

"Let me speak to her."

"Babe, you know damn well Saylor don't want to talk to you."

"Put her on the phone," I ordered. "Now."

The line ended, and I looked at the phone. "Baby, you're so hard... I love your dick," Mercedes continued to have fun on my dick. I let her have her fun, while I dialed Kenni back. This time I called her from my cellphone.

"So because Saylor don't want to get on the phone you hang up on me?" This little bitch was slick as fuck and I could tell that she was up to something.

"Who the fuck you got in the crib, Kenni. Stop fucking playing with me," I barked on the phone. At this point, Mercedes had come and was now sucking the life out my shit so I could nut.

"Nobody except me and Saylor... why the hell you so worried about me? You're the one fucking another bitch. I'm not stupid, Maurice, I could hear clapping in the background!" she yelled.

"I'm gonna deal with your ass when I come home," I told her. A nigga couldn't wait to get home and see if she kept that same energy.

"Ight. Later," she ended the call.

I put my phone on the dresser and held Mercedes head and

fucked her with frustration. Kenni had me pissed and I was taking that shit out on Mercedes's mouth.

After fucking all morning, we decided to get dressed and take Mia out to the zoo. Mercedes wanted a family so bad, so she did the most with taking pictures, holding my hands and kissing me occasionally. To her, this was like a dream come true. Everybody complimented us on how beautiful Mia was, and how she looked just like me and Mercedes both. I kept checking in with Kenni and she was giving me one word answers and taking forever to text me back. She knew I hated when she did shit like that.

"We're supposed to spend time together with Mia and you've been occupied with your phone." Mercedes cut up Mia's chicken nuggets. We were out to eat at some expensive ass restaurant she wanted to try. The food was mediocre and cost a bunch of damn money.

"I know. I'm just trying to keep tabs on Kenni."

Mercedes sighed. "Kenni is not your child, Maurice. She's your girlfriend, not someone you need to be keeping tabs on. Let that girl live her life." She held the cup so Mia could drink her apple juice.

"I didn't ask you shit, Mercedes."

"You're going to lose her. It's bad enough that you beat on that girl. It's crazy that she deals with that." She sucked her teeth.

"You act like I ain't never knocked sense into your ass."

"You got knocked right the fuck back. Maurice, you hit me once and that was the end of us."

"You love rewriting history. So you fucking one of my niggas never happened?"

Mercedes laughed. "Yep, right after you nursed a busted lip

and me a black eye," I laughed because that's exactly how the shit happened.

"Let me worry about my relationship. You worried about her but trying to have a baby with her man."

"I know her man won't stop fucking around on her. Doesn't matter if it's me or someone else, so I might as well get my baby out of it, and some memories for Mia's baby book." She shrugged. "She's only in the position because I stepped out of mine."

"Yeah, you think that. She wifey."

"Why you haven't married her?" she questioned and looked at me for the answer. The question was one I was asked by Juleena – a lot. She always asked if I loved Kenni so much why did I continue to put my hands on her and why haven't I asked her to marry me.

"Don't worry about that. I don't wanna talk about this in front of my daughter," I pinched Mia's cheeks. She giggled while stuffing her face with chicken nuggets. "We did make a beautiful ass baby."

"We did." Mercedes smiled at our daughter. "What is going on with India?"

"What you mean?" I hadn't been really fucking with India since I left her stupid ass house a few weeks ago. After she cried like she couldn't suck me off, I didn't feel like dealing with her cry baby ass. A bitch that couldn't suck dick the way I liked wasn't one I wanted to be near.

"We were supposed to go shopping for the kids and I went by and she was still in the bed. The kids were in their rooms screaming and she had an empty bottle of vodka next to the bed."

"She always got vodka around the crib."

"And you don't see where that's a problem, Maurice?" she

looked at me through squinted eyes. "Me and India grew close because of Mia and her brother. She loves her brother despite how us adults feel about each other. I've always felt like she's an unfit mother. Those kids be dirty sometimes. Kenni is always bringing clothes over for them. Where's the money going?"

I heard what Mercedes was saying and I knew I needed to stay on top of India. I usually came by, fucked, and then was out the door. India had other kids and she didn't raise them. Why did I expect for her to be a good mother to my kids?

"You and her hang out because you like to talk shit about Kenni. Don't try and make it like it's all about the kids."

"Please. Do you really think I spend all my time worried about Kenni? You really think that she's this perfect princess and we all wanna be her. Wrong."

"Yet, you're here with me trying to act like a family."

"She don't have your kids so who is she really trying to be like once she has kids?" she raised her eyebrows. "None of that is important. You really need to be on India's case with those kids."

"I'm gonna pop up on her when I get back to Maryland," I promised.

We continued eating and then hit the mall. Mercedes was in and out all those little kid stores. I remember it was a time when she would buy purses, heels and all the shit that she wanted. Now it was all about our daughter and what she needed. I didn't mind spending the cash to make sure my seed was taken care of. It made me think of Maurice Jr and Mya. I love my kids, even though it seemed like I left everything up to their mothers. I never wanted any of my kids to suffer. It was the reason I worked so hard to make sure shit was good for them. India was going to have to answer some questions and get her shit together. I was going to make sure of it too.

Eight

Haze

KENNI HAD COME into town and we had been kicking it with everybody else. I didn't get a chance to really sit and chill with her one on one again. She and Saylor had been kicking it, and then we would all link together and have drinks. I could tell her mind was somewhere else, and I wanted to sit and talk with her. I remember there was a time when we would just kick it in the staircase, share a blunt, and vent about our problems. She would always vent about her mother and how she's jealous of her, and I would vent about not having money to buy whatever new Jordan that was coming out. Our problems seemed to be so juvenile back then. I wished those problems were the problems I had now.

"Let me head up out of here. I'm meeting Saylor at my crib," Hans got up from the couch and grabbed his wallet off the counter.

We were in the trap counting up money and drinking. It was the first of the month so we always came and counted up the month's money. I ran the stack of money through the money machine and chuckled to myself. Since Saylor been down here I haven't been able to link with my brother. A few times we were supposed to pop in on some of our soldiers and he bailed on my ass each time. The only reason I knew Saylor was here was because Whitney ran into them eating at a restaurant while she was getting her take-out order. When she explained the woman he was with, I knew it was Saylor.

"You real serious about reconnecting with Saylor, huh?"

"I'm not going to front. You both look good together. Shorty compliments you." Kook took a pull from his blunt.

Hans smirked and sat down at the kitchen table. "She something special. I always told you that Saylor was the one. The place we were in life wasn't the right time."

"And you think right now is the right time?" I looked over at him and wrapped the rubber band around the stack of money.

"Yeah. I'm doing better in life and she is too. Why wouldn't right now be the right time?" He looked at me.

"You always acting like you can't be bothered with a woman and how they slow you down. You were pissed when me and Whitney got serious."

"I was pissed because of who her baby father is. Plus, she slowed you down a lot. You used to be out with me and Kook, but now you gotta go home and be a family man."

Hans couldn't stand that me and Whitney were together. "I got responsibilities. I can't be in the streets forever."

"You right. What's going on with you and Kenni? Y'all linked alone yet?" he tried to switch the subject.

I knew he was serious with Saylor when he told me that she

was at his house instead of his condo. Hans never invited anyone to his house. Half the time I met up with him he was always at his condo in the city. For her to be invited to his crib meant this was more than what he was putting on. She had been down here and he didn't tell me nothing. If it wasn't for Whitney, I wouldn't have known she was down here.

"Not besides all of us kicking it together."

"Are you going to kick it with her? You did all this talk about how she was the one that got away," Kook interjected his ass into the conversation again.

"Shut the fuck up."

"All I'm saying is that you were in love with this woman. Now, you got the chance to be all up in her shit and you acting pussy," Hans added.

"I got a girlfriend and she got a man."

"Who?"

"Bridge, nigga."

Hans' jaw tightened and he looked away. "Me and that nigga got beef."

"Silent beef," Kook cackled.

"I was in no condition to come at him with the way I was. I had Haze to worry about and couldn't be selfish. If I would have come at him at that time, I wouldn't be here right now."

"And now you're in a better position... what you going to do about it now?" Kook challenged him. Kook lived on busting his gun and showing people he was in control. He was the rowdy one.

"The fuck you want me to do? Roll up and air his car out?"

"No. Use Kenni as a spy inside of his life. She's with the nigga so she knows how he moves and all that."

I laughed. "I'm not even about to put her in the middle of this shit."

"This nigga tried to kill your brother and you don't wanna help him?" Kook tried to play on my emotions.

He knew how hard it was for both me and Hans when everything went down. I almost lost my brother and had to leave what had been home for us. We always had plans on leaving and it was a done deal, but we basically had to run out the projects and leave almost everything we had behind. As much as I wanted Bridge dead, I didn't think about him because life moved on. At the time it would have been showing up to a gun fight with a knife. Bridge would have killed both of us. I wasn't that same nigga that I used to be.

"Don't do that to him. When it's my time to see Bridge, trust I'm gonna see him." Hans stood up again. "Stop being a pussy and link with Kenni alone. Hit her up and take her on a date."

"Ha. A date," I continued to put money through the machine.

"Yeah. What's wrong with that?"

"Nigga, I got a whole shorty at home. What I look like wining and dining the next woman? I'm not like that."

"Then don't use the word date. Meet up for drinks or something."

"Yeah. I'll see," I replied.

After Kook and Hans left, I put the money away in the safe. Nobody knew about this trap. In fact, it didn't even look like one. We came and went normally and didn't keep late hours. We usually came in the morning and was gone before people started coming home. One time we had someone come knock on the door and ask about attending the HOA meeting. We paid our dues and stored whatever we needed here. Once I looked over everything, I grabbed me a bottle of soda out the fridge and locked up the crib and exited through the garage. I opened the garage and pulled out. My tints were so dark that nobody ever saw who was driving the black Maserati. I always kept the same car when I came over here. Showing up in different cars was a sure way to alert someone that something was up. As far as my neighbors, they thought that me, Kook, and Hans were roommates and traveled often. I didn't give a hell what they thought, I was just glad they weren't in our business.

Grabbing my phone, I called Whitney's cellphone. She had told me that she was going to her mother's crib when we parted ways this morning. "Hey baby. What's up?" she answered.

"Nothing. Just was checking on you. What you doing?"

"I'm heading to Philly with my cousin. She has to go and meet her son's father to get my baby cousin," she explained. "Brittany is still with her dad. He's supposed to drop her off tonight."

"You weren't going to tell me you were heading out the state?"

"Hold on, baby. It's Rod." She quickly clicked over on the other line. I maneuvered through the traffic and waited for her to come back on the other line. "Baby?"

"Yeah."

"Rod says that he's going to keep her for another night. I told him that was fine so you didn't have to deal with Brit."

"You acting like I don't know how to take care of Brittany. He could have dropped her off," I hated when Rod did that shit. He acted like I didn't know how to take care of his daughter. If we wanted to be honest, I took care of his daughter more than he did.

"I'm not saying that you don't know how to take care of her. With him about to have a baby, I know he's not going to get Brittany like that. It's only one night."

"You staying the night in Philly?"

"No, we're driving back. I'll be home late, but I'll be home." She cooed into the phone. I wasn't in the place to receive her flirting.

"Yeah. Ight. Talk to you later," I said.

"Really, Haze?"

"Yeah. You heading out the state and don't think I should know about it. You wanna know if I take a piss at the gas station near the crib. Shit real different."

"I'm a grown ass woman, Haze. You're not my father. I didn't think I had to ask you to go with my cousin."

"Know what? You right. I'm not your father," I ended the call.

Whit called back a few times and I ignored her call while I called Kenni. "Hey, Haze," she answered.

"What's good, Ma? What you up to?"

"I was about to head to the mall. Saylor ditched me to hang with Hans, so I'm alone right now... hold on," she said. A nigga was tired of people putting him on hold. "I'm back. Had to get into the car."

"I knew his ass was running out to be with her. Me and him were together a little while ago." We both laughed. "They must like each other, huh?"

"I mean... it's been a long time coming. Saylor has always had a crush and he's always acted like he liked her. So, I guess it's fate."

"It's fate that I ran into you at Kook's crib?"

"Maybe." She giggled.

"What mall you heading to?"

"Stony point fashion park," she replied.

I looked at my Rolex. "I'm not too far from there. I can meet you there in about twenty."

"You wanna come shopping with me. You do know that I spend hours in the mall, right?"

"Nothing changed from when we were kids. Except, you got the money to do that now," I joked.

"Shut up. Me and Saylor weren't in the mall like that."

"Kings Plaza was the first stop y'all went when you both got some money. Remember that time I went and you spent six hours in there?"

"Alright, you might have a point." She giggled. "I'll be waiting."

"Bet. See you soon."

Whitney had me pissed off and I would be damned if I sat in the crib alone. She expected me to tell her wherever I was going and when it came to her, I found out when I asked. The shit worked both ways. I never lied to her about going out with Kenni. She told me that she wasn't feeling it, and I told her that we were all chilling. I asked a few times if she wanted to kick it with us and she always declined. In her eyes, Kenni was the enemy and trying to break up our relationship. It was crazy that she thought all of this and Kenni just popped into our lives and didn't try to do none of that shit.

It didn't take me long to make it to the mall. Kenni called and told me where she was parked, so I headed in her direction. When I pulled up, she was getting out of her car. Her hair was straightened and hanging down her back. She had on a pair of skin tight jeans, Air Maxes, white baby tee, and a Louis Vuitton messenger bag across her body. She smiled and walked over my whip while securing her car. I hopped out my car and hit the alarm on my car before pulling her into a hug. She smelled like Chanel no.5. Her hair smelled of peaches and everything about her screamed perfection.

"It's about time we kicked it alone," I said after we broke our hug.

She moved her hair to the back and smiled. "All you had to do was ask. Saylor doesn't stay at the hotel with me, so you could have come over and hung with me."

"I may take you up on that offer."

"Can we grab some food first? I haven't had anything to eat and I'm starving," she asked.

"One of my favorite restaurants is in here... you wanna grab food there?"

"You know here more than me. Lead the way."

I grabbed hold of her hand and we made our way through the parking lot to the restaurant. Opening the door, I let her walk in first and grabbed the second door so she could walk through that one too.

"Welcome to Flemings... How many are in the party today?"

"Just two."

"Follow me," the hostess smiled. "How is you guy's day going so far?" she asked, as she walked us to our table.

"Pretty good," Kenni replied.

When we got to the table, she placed our menus in our hands and smiled again. "Your waitress will be with you soon. Enjoy your time at Flemings." She walked away and I looked across the table at Kenni.

"All of this looks so good." She licked her lips. "I don't even know what I want to decide on."

"Get it all."

"There's no way that I'm going to be able to eat all of this food. This seafood tower looks and sounds good."

"Welcome to Flemings. My name is Sassy and I'll be your waitress this afternoon. What can I get you guys to drink?"

"Can I have peach tea." Kenni told her.

She jotted down on the pad. "And you, Sir."

"Let me get a sprite."

"While I'm here... any appetizers looking good to you both?"

"The seafood tower," I told her.

"Great choice. I'll put that in and then come back to get your main course order." She turned and headed toward the kitchen.

"You didn't have to get that... we can go half on the bill." When she said that shit, it lowkey made me tight.

"I'm not hurting for money, Kenni... I'm not gonna be in here spending money I don't have. Lose that broke Haze out of your memory. I'm not him anymore," I warned her.

I could tell she was a little embarrassed before she looked away. "I didn't mean it that way. It would be rude for me to say I wanted food and expect you to foot the bill. Has nothing to do with you being broke."

"I know when I left we had got into it and you chose to go with Bridge... I wasn't in the best place and I know you always kept me at a distance because I was a broke nigga."

"I was shallow back then." She sighed. "I'm sorry for treating you the way I did. Back then, I was so concerned on trying to get out my mama's house and having the best gear."

"It is what it is."

"No it isn't. We were best friends. You've always been there when me and my mother got into it. I could always turn to you and you would be there without a doubt and I fucked that up for some new nigga that rolled on the block."

"You're happy and shit. None of that matters anymore. We were eighteen and didn't know what the fuck we were doing."

"I remember the night you told me that you wanted me to

come with you to Virginia. Being honest, I wished I would have gone with you and Hans. My life would have been different."

I was confused. The Kenni I knew wanted all the things she had now. She wanted the drug dealer nigga, shopping sprees and luxury cars. Last I checked, that was the life that she now had and she sounded like this wasn't what she wanted.

"This was what you wanted. You drive a Benz most bitches want. That bag you're wearing is a few stacks."

"Haze, money isn't all that it's cracked up to be." She flipped through the menu again, avoiding eye contact with me. "All this money and shopping doesn't mean a damn thing to me."

"Ight, you being real vague with me. It's me. I'm the same Haze that you told you got your period in school and I gave you my sweater to wrap around you because your mama said she wasn't coming up to the school. Ain't nothing changed except the year. What's up with you?"

The waitress came back over. "Are you guys ready to order?"

"I'll do the double breast chicken," Kenni ordered.

"And I'll do the same." I usually got the steak and had a bunch of modifications that I made to my meal, but right now I wanted to get down to what was good with Kenni.

"I'll go and put those in right now. Any drinks?"

"Moscato, please," Kenni added.

"What size glass?" she countered.

"Bring the bottle," I told her.

"Well... okay. I'll bring that to you," she replied and took back off again. I prayed the next time she brought her ass over here that she would just sit down what we ordered and be quiet.

"We shouldn't be getting into this right now. Let's just enjoy."

"I'm not going to be able to chill and enjoy," I looked at my phone and Whit was calling me again. Ignoring her call, I powered my phone off and turned my attention to Kenni.

"Everyone thinks me and Bridge are perfect. Things haven't been right for some time, and I continue to put up with this relationship."

"Relationships aren't perfect. I just argued with my girl before coming to meet up with you... that's the thing about relationships."

"You haven't had three babies on your girlfriend and you damn sure don't put your hands on her," she revealed.

Kenni didn't disclose much about she and Bridge's relationship. All I knew was that they were still together and that was that. I was surprised that they had lasted that long. Kenni got bored easily, so I expected her to move onto the next nigga right away.

"He put his hands on you?"

"Bridge has always put his hands on me. I'm always nursing a broken nose, black eye, or my favorite, broken rib." She tried to make light of her situation.

"Ma, that shit isn't funny. Why you even still with the nigga?" hearing that he put his hands on her made me pissed as fuck. All these years I liked to think that she was somewhere living her best life, not being abused.

"I know it's not funny. I'm sorry, I just can't help but to laugh... who would have ever thought that I would be in this situation? I've always been outspoken and didn't put up with shit and look at me now."

"None of that matters. That nigga don't have no business

putting his hands on a woman. I don't give a fuck what you've done. A nigga isn't supposed to hit a woman."

She removed her hair from her face. "When I ran into you, I had actually ran away. Literally had to beg his cousin to come save me because I found out that he was fucking with another bitch. Then, he has the nerve to put his hands on me."

This shit was crazy. She told me everything that was going on between them. From the babies he had with India and some other chick, to random chicks he fucked and she ended up finding out about.

"Right before he left. I saw another baby he probably had. He lied and told me he didn't know the woman, but I'm not stupid."

"Damn. I can't believe that he got a baby with India."

"And you do too. India's son looks just like you."

I laughed. "She tried to pin her baby on me. Me and India used to fuck, but that was it. Her son's father is some Spanish nigga from Harlem."

"Who hasn't India fucked?" she sighed. "You sure? That little boy looked like you," she questioned again.

India had told me that her son was mine. At first I believed it. He had my same curly hair, darkened complexion, and his eyes were similar to mine. Hans was the one who told me to be smart and get the baby tested. He handed me some money and we went down to the health center and the baby wasn't mine. If I had a son by India, he would have been coming with me. India's ass was an unfit mother who felt like her life was more important than a child's life. I was surprised that Bridge even ran up in there and had a baby by her. Everybody knew that she just wanted a baby by a nigga with money so she could live off that money. I guess dreams did come true. She ended up having

Bridge's baby and I knew she was milking him for whatever he had.

"Oh really? I thought he was your son."

"I strapped up each time with her. When she came to me about the baby I believed her, but Hans made me get a DNA test. India is a hoe and she's always going to be one."

"That's something I can agree on."

"Let me ask you something?"

"What?"

"Why are you still with him? He fucking abuses you and disrespects you. You've got to know that you're worth more than that."

I could tell she was battling with if she wanted to be honest, or if she wanted to leave the subject alone. "He provides for me. Who do I have? My mama is god knows where, my brothers are in Georgia and they have a beautiful life. Who do I really have?"

"Saylor. When I asked you about her, you said you both are sisters. She's not going nowhere. What happened to that? Saylor would drop anything to be there for you."

"I'm a grown woman, Haze. Saylor shouldn't have to come to my rescue. She has her own life and I don't want her having to drop things to be there for me."

"You'd rather deal with this then?"

"I've gotten used to it. He's not all bad."

"Here you go." She sat this huge seafood tower in the middle of us and then poured some wine into the glass and sat it beside Kenni.

"Thanks," I told her. "Answer my question."

"No, I wouldn't rather deal with this. Bridge provides for me. Before, I was fishing for my next meal and trying to figure out how I was going to get clothes. You know my mama, and you know she didn't give a damn about neither of her kids. Bridge isn't perfect, but he has been the most consistent person in my life. He has provided for me."

Slamming my hand on the table, the few patrons seated near us looked over at us. "And in the same breath you're telling me that he fucking puts his hands on you. It doesn't matter that you're eating lobster with a busted lip, long as he provided the food, right?"

Tears fell down her cheeks and she grabbed her purse. "Haze, that's not your place. I got to go." She gathered her things and took off out the restaurant.

I stood up and told the waitress to wait and chased behind her. When I got outside, she was already stepping off the curb to head into the parking lot.

"Kenni, wait," I walked over to her and she turned around so quick that her hair slapped her in the face.

"Haze, honestly, my situation is fucked up already. I don't need someone screaming it out in a restaurant. I've been dealing with Bridge, and I know what I'm doing. Let's just go back to living our lives and act like we haven't run into each other again!" she screamed and stormed into the parking lot.

"Kenni!" I called and she ignored me.

I wanted to chase behind her and tell her that I didn't mean it. Except, I had the manager waiting at the door like I was trying to dine and ditch. Hearing how Bridge had someone as precious as Kenni, and he put his hands on her and disrespected her pissed me off.

"Calm the fuck down," I said when I walked through the door. It killed me how I came in here all the time and these dickheads were acting like I was about to run and ditch the bill. "I come in this bitch all the time. Get me the bill and pack all this shit to-go," I barked.

"Sorr, Sir—"

"Keep all that shit to yourself... I don't want to hear that shit. A black man runs after his girl and y'all acting like I'm stealing." White people in the movies did that shit all the time and you didn't see them chasing behind them.

After paying the bill, I grabbed the two brown bags and headed to the car. I wasn't about to waste this food. Kook sent me a text message about some business we needed to handle, so I put the food in the back seat and headed to meet him.

 Nine

Kenni

I was so irritated and embarrassed that I drove straight to the hotel with no music on. My thoughts were loud enough and I didn't need to hear anything else. Haze had embarrassed the shit out of me in that restaurant. I understood that he didn't understand, hell, most people didn't. However, he didn't have to do all of that in the restaurant. Me and Bridge's relationship wasn't for everybody and I understood his reaction. How else was he supposed to act? Bridge put his hands on me and had no problems with it. He would yell it out if he felt the need in a store if I did something that he didn't like. Still, it wasn't Haze's position to yell my business for the entire restaurant to hear. I had never felt so hot and angry as I did at the moment. Leaving him at the restaurant was the best thing to do. If I didn't, I was going to hurt his feelings and that was the last thing that I wanted to do.

That whole incident had bothered me so much that I had been sitting in the same spot since I got into my hotel room. It was now nine at night and I hadn't turned on the TV, removed my sneakers, or used the bathroom. Haze really set something off inside of me and I didn't know how to deal with it. The old Haze, I wouldn't have cared what he thought. This new and improved Haze was different. He wasn't the same Haze that let me just vent and agreed with everything. This Haze was different. He was vocal and didn't care what came out of his mouth. It was a nice change. Haze had always been a push over, so to him standing his ground and being vocal actually made me happy. What made me sad was that he was using it on me. I never imagined that my life would be like this. I hated to even think of myself as a battered woman. In my eyes, I was strong. I fought back each time Bridge put his hands on me. The way Haze looked at me when I revealed that Bridge put his hands on me made me ashamed. He looked at me like I was a hurt fragile bird. It bothered me and seeing how upset he got shocked me too.

I looked down at my ringing phone and picked up soon as I saw Esma's name pop across the screen. "Hey Nana, what's up?"

I didn't see Esma as much as I used to. Even with me not seeing her, we spoke every week on the phone. She prayed for me and didn't pass judgement on me. She was much easier to talk to than Saylor at times. Where she could tell me I was being stupid and constantly tell me that each time we spoke, she didn't. She allowed me to make my own decisions, even if they were horrible ones.

"Kenni, how are you doing, mamas?"

"I'm good. Taking it one day at a time... is everything

alright?" I questioned. With her being in New York alone, I worried about her. Especially with Saylor here.

"I'm glad. Your mother reached out to me," she started. I hadn't spoken to my mother since the day she beat me down like a grown woman in the streets, and I left.

There was no need for me to ever speak to her again. She treated me so horribly. I think it was part of the reason I allowed people to treat me like shit and didn't value the good ones.

"You did?"

"Yes. I've kept in contact with Terri over the years. You know my number has never changed. I made Saylor switch my house number right on over in her house." She laughed. "Her phone numbers has changed, but she still called me from time to time to let me know how she was doing."

"Didn't think she cared about anybody other than herself."

"Your mother is a very difficult woman to understand, Kenni." She sighed. "She has a lot of hurt and anger that she has never dealt with, and she transferred that onto her children." Esma explained. I didn't want to hear any excuse as to why my mother couldn't be a mother. The shit she had done to me as my mother was unacceptable. She constantly chose her niggas over her kids and fought me like a grown bitch in the street.

"Nana, I really don't want to get into that right now. Terri made her decisions and now she has to live with them."

"She's dying, Kenni," she blurted.

"D...dying?" I stammered. How?"

Esma sighed into the phone. "She has liver failure... she doesn't have much time and reached out to me. She wants to see you, Kenni." She told me.

"I don't know if I'm ready to see her again."

"You don't want to regret saying goodbye to her. Despite how you feel, get your closure, baby. She's at Methodist hospital in Brooklyn. I told her I would pass the message onto you and let you decide what you wanted to do with it."

"Thank you, Nana. I'm not sure I want to see her. The last time we saw each other still gives me chills. Then, she just gave up her rights for the boys and doesn't even check on them."

"Baby, I'm not forcing you to do anything that you don't want to do. This is your life and it's up to you what you want to do. I gave you the information and it's whatever you want." Someone knocked on my room door.

"Thanks, Nana. I'll think about it. Someone is at my door right now...Can I call you later?"

"Of course. I love you," she said.

"Love you too."

We ended the call and I went to the door. Haze was standing there with two brown paper bags in his hands. "How does one say I'm an asshole and I'm sorry in Spanish?"

"I think it sounds better in English," I leaned on the door. "And what is in the bags?" I eyed the paper bag.

"The food you left at the restaurant. I had them package it up and brought it home to sit in the fridge while I handled some business. You gonna let me in?"

I folded my arms and looked at him. "Hmm."

"Yo, stop playing with me," he barged into the hotel room and I closed the door behind us.

I leaned on the hotel door with my arms still folded. "Why are you here? Clearly you're bothered by my relationship and what goes on in it."

He put the bags down on the counter and turned to look at me. "I'm sorry. I shouldn't have called you out like that and told people your business. It wasn't my place and I apologize."

He walked near me. "Pleaseeeeee. See, you got a nigga begging for your forgiveness."

Seeing Haze beg was something different for me. When it came to Bridge admitting that he was wrong, it never happened. It was always the same shit when it came to him. When we first got together he used to apologize and try and make it work. That was because he was trying to win me over. Now, I didn't know who the man was that I shared a home with. I knew one thing for certain, he wasn't the same man that I had fell in love with.

"Alright. You can stop begging," I laughed and went over to the table. When I stormed out of the restaurant, my mouth watered because I really wanted to eat what we had ordered. "You really had them package this food up?"

"Hell yeah. Just because I have money doesn't mean I'm about to waste that shit. Plus, I knew your stubborn ass was hungry and I planned to bring it over later."

"Well, I appreciate that. I haven't had someone do something nice like that for me in a long time."

"Don't mention it." He pulled the containers up and I grabbed them and placed them in the microwave. The hotel room I was in had a small kitchenette. I hated saying in hotel rooms that didn't have a microwave or a fridge.

While I heated the food, Haze sat down at the small metal table and looked over at me. "What?" I blushed.

"You're beautiful as fuck. You know that?"

"Where is this coming from?"

"Nowhere. I've always felt like that. You were beautiful then, and now you're even more beautiful."

I moved my hair out of my face and continued to blush. The way he was staring at me made me do the corny cheese smile. It was different hearing that I was beautiful from Haze.

His compliment didn't come with anything. He didn't compliment me because I had caught him fucking another bitch, or because he brought another baby into our relationship. He was complimenting me because he felt that I was really beautiful. It was easy to lose your way when you're in a toxic relationship like I was in with Bridge. I used to be so confident.

"It's been a while since I've heard that. Thank you."

"You know you're beautiful. Shit, you used to scream that shit any time you were given the chance. What happened to that Kenni?"

"She died," I revealed. "I haven't felt like her in so long that I buried her away somewhere." My confidence used to be on a high. I never needed a nigga's validation. With my body, face, and personality, I knew that I was the shit. Anything a nigga added was a bonus. I made them look good. I was the dime on their arms that every nigga wanted. The thing about me, I didn't fuck around with any nigga. You had to bring something to my table to even be worth being seen with me. I missed that Kenni.

Haze got up from the table and walked over to me. He put his hand on the side of my waist and looked down at me. "You gotta know your worth, ma. I can show you your worth, but you gotta know it first. You've allowed that man to strip you of everything. Your worth, confidence, voice and everything else."

This was why I left earlier. He caused me to think and cry. I cried because when I sat and thought about my relationship with Bridge, I grew sad. I was sad because I was living in hell and didn't know how to pull myself out. People had their outside opinions and Saylor lent her help. Still, I wanted to be able to pull myself out of this hell. Moving from one person who took care of me to another wasn't the way I wanted to live. I wanted to be able to say that I pulled myself out of the hell that I was living in. That I was able to leave Bridge and be free, all while taking care of myself. Fast cars, clothes, and money was a must when I looked at a man. I just wanted a man who cared about me and put my feelings as a priority. I wanted a man who would never raise his hand to harm me, and a man who put my happiness as a priority.

"You letting that fuck nigga take away who you are, Ken. You've never been one of those girls who allowed a nigga to do whatever. I remember you slapped the fuck outta that nigga Tim in the building when he mushed you in the head, and that nigga was just playing with you. You've always stood up for yourself because you had no other choice."

"I had to stand up for myself because who else was going to do it? My mama wasn't concerned about protecting me. It was something I had to do since being young."

"What's your excuse now?"

I broke out in tears and he pulled me into his arms. "He was supposed to protect me. Haze, he promised that he would protect, love, and care for me," I continued to sob when I thought about all the promises that Bridge had promised me. I let that guard down and figured I didn't have to be so head strong because I had someone to protect me. Bridge was supposed to protect and care for me. Instead, he was the one who I needed protection from. He was the one who put his hands on me, lied, and brought more hurt than he knew on me.

"Chill, I don't like to see you crying. Ken, you control the narrative. You're the only one who can stop what he's doing. I can offer you money, an escape route and handle him, but at the end of the day you'll still go back to him. I need you to tell him when enough is enough." He held my face in hands and looked down into my eyes. "You hear me?"

"I hear you. I hear you." He wiped the tears that fell down my cheeks and then kissed me on the forehead. Then, he kissed my nose, until he landed on my lips. I kissed him back and wrapped my arms around his neck. I felt so protected being in Haze's arms. In one way or another, he had always been my protector. Always somewhere looking from afar, but still making sure that I was always good.

"I don't want you hurt, Ma. Hearing that shit earlier took me to a dark place. The thought of that nigga putting his hands on you does something to my spirit." He continued to stare me in the eyes. "I've always loved you and never stopped. You've always been the one that I wanted to be with, Kenni. Always."

Standing on my toes, I kissed him on the lips. "I don't deserve you," I told him when we broke our kiss.

It was true. Haze was a good man and I could have had him in my life. We probably would have been happy, had a kid or two, and I wouldn't have gone through all this hurt and pain. Except, I was too caught up in money and what a nigga could do for me to give him the time of day.

"Let me decide that." He picked me up and carried me to where the bed was. He laid me down on the bed and leaned over me and showered me with kisses. He was gentle and his lips felt like small clouds showering my body. "You're beautiful. I want you to know that you're fucking beautiful to me," he leaned over me and looked me in the eyes.

"My mom is dying," I blurted. It had been sitting on my mental since I ended the call with Esma. Why did I care so much? Terri treated me like shit the moment I came out of her. When I strained my brain, I could never come up with good times between us. Maybe it was when she was showing me how to roll a blunt, or when she showed me how to finesse niggas and to give my virginity away to the nigga with the most money. I guess those were considered good times.

Haze's expression turned serious, but he still leaned over me in the bed and stared into my eyes. "How do you feel?"

His question was so simple yet took me by surprise. Hearing those four simple words took my words away. Nobody ever asked how I was doing. Saylor always called but tried not to get too deep into what I was going through. In her mind, I needed to leave. She didn't want to hear about what I was going through. I knew that I had to leave, still, that didn't mean I didn't have the right to express what I was going through.

He wiped the tear that fell down my cheek. "I don't know why I'm so bothered by her dying. I shouldn't care, right?" I searched his eyes for answers.

He rubbed my face and kissed me on the lips. "I can't tell you how to feel. Terri is a unique woman and she wasn't my favorite person, but that's your moms. How I feel and you feel are two different things."

"How did you feel when your mom was dying?"

"Man... hurt, crushed, and useless."

"Useless?"

"Yeah. There wasn't anything that I could do. I had to sit there and watch her wither away, all while trying to still be a mother to me and Hans."

"If you could switch, would you?"

"Hell yeah. I would have given up anything to have her. Even now, I would give all that I have to bring her back to me," he explained. Even though it had been years since his mother passed away, you could still see the hurt in his eyes. I could still see that she was a sore subject to talk about. "Even with how I felt about my mother… it's not the same as you and Terri. How I feel isn't necessary how you would feel about your moms."

"I know. Esma called and told me right when you knocked on the door. It's been rolling through my head since and she wants to see me."

"You going to see her?"

"I haven't seen her in years or heard from her. It was like she was dead in some weird way. Even Rakim hadn't heard from her. It was like she vanished. Why does she want to see me now?"

"Maybe she wants to make things right. You're going to regret not going to see her. I'm not saying you have to kiss, make-up or even forgive her… just go and see her to make peace for yourself." He messed with a pair of my lose hair. "My pops died and on his death bed he wanted me to forgive him for being a shit ass father. Even on his death bed I couldn't forgive him. He wanted to leave this earth knowing that he had been forgiven, and I couldn't even give him that. Thinking back, I should have forgave him… Not for him, but for me."

"Wow," I messed with the pieces of hair that fell from his shoulder. "I want to see her. I think I need to make this peace. Even if she doesn't die until two years later, I want to know that I saw her, made peace and closed that chapter in my life."

I was part to blame for my life decisions, but I also held my mother responsible too. She was supposed to teach me the tools I needed to conquer this world as a woman. Instead, she was too jealous of her own daughter to do those things. All she wanted from me was to raise her children that she laid down and had. Then again, how could she teach me? She wasn't given the tools to be a woman. She was a failed student, just like I was.

"Then make it happen. Make that peace and gracefully

close that chapter." He pecked me on the lips. "You going to call Rakim and tell him?"

"I don't think I should. She's caused so much drama and abuse in the boy's life that they don't need anymore. They're happy and living a great life. She left them and never reached out, so why reach out and interrupt their lives now with that negative news? The boys don't even ask about her, and Keith doesn't even remember her."

"You know best." He stared into my eyes.

"What?" I blushed.

"I want you in the worst way. Can't even believe I'm in this hotel with you... no lie, a nigga used to dream about a life with you."

His words and the way they fell off his tongue caused me to blush. His voice brought me tranquility. I could listen to him talk forever and never get tired. "Stop playing."

"No funny shit. Kenni, you don't know how much I wanted you back then."

"I wish I paid more attention. I'm sorry."

He kissed me on the lips. "What was done, was done. It's how we move forward that counts."

"God, you're so positive."

"Took a lot. I used to be angry. Had to check that shit and find my own peace. Not much can take me out of that."

"Except Bridge," I giggled. "You were slamming that hand on that table pretty hard. Sure you didn't get a splinter?" he rolled to the side and pulled me on top of him.

"That nigga was too old for you from the jump. He was a fucking predator looking for a young chick to take advantage of," he voiced.

"I know," I admitted.

He kissed me again and then rubbed his fingers down my

lips. "So fucking beautiful. God took his time when he made you, Ken."

"What are we doing, Haze? I'm with Bridge and you have a girlfriend. We can't fall into something because one of our hearts will end up broken."

He looked me in the eyes. "There's no need to put a title on a vibe. I know I want you, and I know I'll get you. On my end, I'm going to get my shit together so I could have you the right way. Wanna make me a promise?"

"What?"

"That you'll do your part to get your shit together so that I could get you," I looked down at him and nodded my head.

"K." We kissed and I laid down on his chest. We forgot about the food, and just laid on the bed in silence. I know our minds were both going crazy. Even with my mind going crazy, this feeling felt amazing. Something that I could get used to.

Ten

Saylor

I HAD BEEN HOME a couple weeks. Me and Hans still spoke
every day and night before I went to bed. It was something
about that man that set my soul on fire. Every emotion I had
ever felt, he opened them up. And, he never had to try hard.
Hans was himself and even being himself was enough for me.
More than enough. We had deep conversations that would
cause your toes to crawl. The way he stared into my eyes when
he spoke and held his stare turned me on. I loved that he didn't
see me as some fragile woman. He saw me as his equal. When
he spoke business, he didn't leave the room, or try and brush
me off like I was some air head woman. He spoke to me with so
much respect that I got goose bumps. Then, he had this silly
side with him. A man so hardened in the streets, but gentle in
the sheets was a dream. Hans was a thug when he had to be
one. When he crossed the threshold of his home, he was a

different person. He was smart, funny and caring. Hans was the type of person to give you the shirt off his back. It was what made me fall for him even more.

"How long you going to take to check the damn door? The flowers I sent you gonna be dead by now," he said.

I was in my office going over rent payments for the month and we were talking about nothing. That's how all our conversations were. We could just sit on the phone talking about the air. As long as we were talking, it didn't matter what the conversation was about. I was about to respond when I saw Brix's new number pop across the screen on the other line.

"Fine. Let me take this call and I'll go get them from the front," I told him and quickly switched lines.

After I left Brix at his hotel, we hadn't spoken much. He sent me a text message with his new number. Other than that, we didn't talk how we used to. What was there to speak about? He was never going to leave Juleena. With the way that she was, she wasn't going to give him up. Even if he did leave her, she would always be an issue in any relationship he got himself into. Juleena was more in love with Brix than he was with her. I knew it and everyone around them knew it.

"Hey Brix... what's up?"

"Just checking on you," he replied.

Rolling my eyes, I made my way to the front of the house. "I'm good. Getting some work done," I stopped by the kitchen and grabbed some banana chips off the counter. "You?"

"'Bout to pick the boys up from school. I miss you."

"Brix, don't do this."

"For real. I really miss you. I'm thinking about coming to New York next week," he mentioned.

"Oh yeah. For what?"

"You."

I opened the front door and kneeled down. "Brix, you don't need to be coming to New York for me. We need some time ap—" I stopped when I noticed a pair of Timberland constructions standing in front of the flowers. I was so busy into my conversation that I hadn't bothered to pay attention to what was in front of me. Looking up, I smiled so hard when I saw Hans standing there with a gift box in his hand. "Let me call you back," I quickly ended the call before he could even say anything else.

"Hans!!!" I screamed and jumped into his arms. "What are you doing here?" I kissed him on the lips and screamed in his air. The gift box in his hand wasn't a concern to me.

He walked in the house carrying me. Nana came out and looked at all the commotion. "What is going on out here?" My grandmother knew Hans from the neighborhood. She always kept an eye on Haze and Hans, especially after their mother died. My grandmother did that with all the neighborhood boys. "Hans, is that you?"

"Saylor, get your big self-off him so that I can see," she swatted me on the back and I started shaking my butt on him. I missed seeing him every day, so this surprise was something I welcomed.

"How you doing, Ms. Esma?" he gently put me down and handed me the gift box. I held the box and watched as he hugged and kissed her on the cheek.

"Boy, do you know how worried I was about you boys? I asked around and nobody could give me a straight answer."

"We're sorry. We needed new beginnings," he kept it short.

"When Saylor told me that you both reconnected I was happy as ever." She smiled at me, then up at him.

"Yeah, Saylor makes a ni... me happy," he caught himself before he cursed in front of her.

"How long are you staying? I'll make a dinner tonight so we can catch up on things," she clapped her hands together.

With just the two of us being here she didn't get to cook big dinners like she used to in the past. "That's up to Saylor," he smirked and then looked at me.

"Either way, your butt is going to sit still for dinner tonight." She hugged him again. "I'm going to run to the grocery store and grab some things for dinner."

"You know I can't tell you no," he replied.

My grandmother headed to the kitchen to take inventory of what she had. Hans turned to me and I couldn't wipe the smile off my stupid ass face. "What are you doing here?"

"I can't come see you?"

"You can.... This is just a surprise. A good one. Come on," I nodded for him to follow me into my office.

When we got to my office, he looked around, then turned to look me up and down. "Who the fuck is Brix?"

"Somebody I used to mess with." There was no need to lie. He had been honest about everything, and it was only right for me to return that same respect by being truthful.

"Used to, or are you still fucking him?"

"I saw him the last time I was in Virginia."

"Oh, he from out there? Which part," I could tell from the vein in his neck that this conversation was bothering him.

"No, he's from Maryland. I used to work with him and we got close. We ended things years ago and just reconnected recently," I explained.

"Shorty, no nigga 'bout to drive to Virginia for nothing... Ya'll fucking. Let me know now if this is what we're doing."

I walked over to him and put my arm around his waist as best as I could. Looking up at him, I smirked. "Is Hans jealous?"

"Stop playing with me, Saylor. I got some bitches that have been dying for me to drop some dick off in their draws. I thought we were focused on us, so let me know what we doing so I can move accordingly."

When I saw that he was serious, I took a step back and looked at him. "Are you serious right now?"

"Dead ass serious," he replied.

"Me and Brix had something going on back then. We've spoke a few times and met up, but we're not fucking."

"Then what's the point of meeting up with him and talking, Saylor?" he sat down in one of the chairs in front of my desk. "All I'm trying to do is figure out what the fuck is going on."

"I don't know. What we had was intense... like, I lost myself for a while after we ended things. I relived the whole situation over again. "He hurt me."

"And what did you tell me? You told me that you didn't want to be hurt again. Fuck you even talking with this clown for?"

I sat down in the chair beside him and sighed. "I love what we have, Hans. I do. Yet, I don't know what we have."

"Because we didn't put a label on shit, you wanna go and talk to the next nigga? A label that important to you?"

I screwed my face up. "You know me, and you know I'm not like that at all. Brix has nothing to do with us having a label. I was talking to him before me and you crossed paths. I just want to know what we're doing. I'm tired of being in relationships where I don't know what we're doing, then it ends... you know."

He gently took my hand. "I wanna be with you, Shorty. You're the only woman that I want to see and want the world to know that you're mine. I'm not kicking it with you, I'm trying to build with you." He kissed my hand.

"I also don't want you to say it because I asked."

"Have I ever done anything because someone asked? Why you think I'm here? I haven't been up here in four years and look where I'm at."

I climbed out the chair into his. My body was so small against his that he swallowed me up whole. "So, you wanna be my man?"

"Nah, I am your man," he corrected me. "All I'm asking is for you not to disrespect me. I don't want you out here having me looking crazy."

"Doesn't the woman say that?"

"Yeah. You got me out here acting like a little bitch behind you. Whatever you and this nigga Brick talking about, dead that shit."

"It's Brix, babe," I giggled. "I'll meet up with him and end things. This is something that I should do in person."

"Yeah, just do that shit. Any other nigga I should be concerned about?" I didn't want to mention Darren because he needed me. His wife was doing her thing and not concerned about him. In her defense, she had all rights to live her life. She carried his children and he turned around and cheated on her each time he crossed the state lines. Me and Darren didn't have a romantic relationship. He was lonely and needed a familiar face to visit during his time. Bridge didn't send money or see his cousin. He answered his calls when he felt like it. That enough showed what kind of nigga that he was.

"No. Just Brix. Now, let's discuss how long you staying? Don't you have work to handle?" I kissed him on the neck. After not having sex for years, I craved Hans' dick. Sex between us was intense and pleasing. It was like we both were in competition to please the other.

"I can handle what I need from here. How long I stay is up to you." He kissed me on the lips and spread my legs. His fingers dipped into my pussy and swirled around like he was trying to spread the sugar around in his lemonade.

"Until I tell you to leave."

He licked his fingers and then started massaging my clit again. I tossed my head back and enjoyed the sensation that he was providing. "Oh, word? You gonna tell me to dip when you want."

"N... no baby... I want you to stay.. Don't leave me," I quietly moaned.

"Aright, now," we heard my grandmother's voice and I closed my legs and sat normally on his lap. "I'm going to head to the store," she said when she rounded the corner.

"Okay. Please be safe," I told her, like I always told her.

"Alright," I blew a sigh of relief when she didn't argue me down like she always did. When I heard the door chime and close, I looked back at Hans.

"See, you almost got us caught."

My grandmother lived in the basement apartment in the house. She refused to move unless I gave her some independence, so I renovated down there. She had everything she could ever need. There was no need for her to come up here. Even with her own apartment, I loved when she came and cooked in my kitchen. My grandmother was my world, so I didn't mind her company. With Hans being here, I had to make sure to lock that bottom lock on the door in the basement. I planned to fuck him all over this house and I didn't need my grandmother catching me in the act.

"She'll probably stay in her apartment more now that you're here."

"Nah, I want her to act like I'm not here. There's a time and place for everything. Trust, I'm gonna fuck you on that piano." He winked, as I went to get the box.

"So you've already been plotting."

"Man, I've been plotting on fucking the shit out of you since you left weeks ago. I missed you, yo."

I smiled so wide. Hearing that made me so happy. "You did?"

"Yeah."

"I missed you too."

I sat back on his lap and opened the box up. "The five love languages," I read the title of the book.

I loved to read. It didn't matter what it was, I read. I think I was one of the few people on my block that still got a newspaper delivered, and actually read it. Hans was a reader too. When I went into his office in his home, he had a bunch of books and some with little holders in them, which told me he was still reading the book. A man that read was so sexy to me.

"I read it a while back and learned a lot about it."

"You were married?"

"Nah. I've had enough fucked up relationships. Some woman was reading it while I was grabbing gas and I ended up buying it. It's a good ass read."

"Thank you, Hans. I've heard about this book, but never thought to pick it up. I thought it was for married people."

"It's for relationships. Here's the thing, I'm falling in love with you. What happens after I've fallen? So many people fall in love and then that's when shit hits the fan. I want to fall in love and stay in love. After the time we spent together and the shit we did, it opened me up to the possibility of being in a relationship. I slept on this shit for many nights until I grabbed this book and decided I was going to give it to you in person and ask you to be my woman."

"I'm going to start it tonight," I hugged him. "Thank you."

"You're welcome."

We sat in my office cuddled up and just being in each other's space. Weeks had passed and we haven't saw each other. We spoke on the phone, however, that wasn't the same. It wasn't enough, at least for me. I craved to be near him and smell his sent. I wanted to hear his soft snores, or the grind of his teeth in the middle of the night. It was him who I craved and wanted to be near. It had been a long time since I had felt this way about a man. A man that made me want to be vulnerable, submissive and allow him to take control. It's been a while since I've trusted a man to do those things. It was nice to feel emotions and feelings I felt coming from someone else other than me. It was a mutual feeling that we both had for each other.

"You ever thought about having kids?" Hans asked. We were in Soho having dinner at this small restaurant that a friend of his owned.

When he asked me about going out, I shrugged it off. Besides running my businesses, I didn't get out much. My only friend was in Maryland, and I could have food and drinks in my own home. When he kept insisting that we go out, I got dressed and we headed here. It was a nice low-key vibe with burnt orange and gold accents. The mahogany tables and chairs added to the décor. Sticking my fork into my piece of roasted chicken, I looked up at him.

"I have." The thought of children scared me. Since I lost my baby, I hadn't really thought of having any more children. Each time the thought passed my mind, I rubbed it out of my memory. The last time that I was pregnant, I had felt whole. Although I was young, worried and scared, somehow my baby brought me some peace.

"And?" he took a sip of his drink while looking at me. "You gonna elaborate or continue poking around your plate?"

I sat my fork down. "I lost a baby a few years ago. The thought crosses my mind, but it's not something I give a lot of thought."

"I'm sorry."

"It's not your fault. It wasn't the right time."

He reached across the table and took my hand into his. "Are kids something that you really want, Saylor?"

I hadn't really thought about it. The reason I got pregnant the first time was because I wasn't careful. It wasn't like I was trying for a baby or anything. Me and Darren weren't careful and I ended up carrying his baby. Kids were cute, and because I was a woman I felt like that had to happen.

"I haven't really thought about it. When I got pregnant it was an accident. It wasn't like I was looking to have kids."

"Being completely honest, I think we need to throw shit on the table. Being up front about things we want avoids either of us ending up with a broken heart."

"I agree."

"I want kids. I want like four of them muthafuckas." He stared me in the eyes. "I want to be married, someday. Do I want to get married before kids? Nah."

"I don't want you to give up on me. This whole thing with us scares me because it seems like it's moving too fast, and everything is going too good."

Hans had been at the house for a week, and although I never wanted to admit it to him, I never wanted him to leave. He made waking up to him every morning so worth it. Sharing my huge master suite with him felt like we were married. Every night while he watched the game I would pull out my book and read. It felt so right with him. So right that I was dragging my ass when it came to meeting with Brix. Brix had hurt me, but I didn't want to hurt him back. With all he had going on, the last thing I wanted was to knock him lower.

"We've known each other our entire life. The only thing is that time has passed, which it does. Everything is happening the way that it's supposed to. I'm not saying I want kids tomorrow. I'm saying I want kids in the future. I just want you to know what I want so it's not a surprise later down the line."

"I don't think I want to be married."

"Okay... and why is that?"

"When people get married shit always goes wrong."

"That's why you're reading the book I got you. I don't give a fuck why other people shit goes left when they're married. I'm worried about us working on not ever getting to that place. I said I probably wanted to have kids before getting married because marriage is a big step."

"Kids are an even bigger step. You can divorce in marriage; you can't kill a damn baby."

He laughed. "Not to me. Your kids grow up and eventually leave the nest. You gotta have a personal life, right? My kids will be loved regardless if I'm married or not."

"I guess."

"On the real, I want this. I've never wanted a relationship more than I've wanted this one. This one was blessed from the Most High."

"Hans, really?"

"Yeah. He brought you back to me for a reason and told me not to fuck it up."

I laughed. "He cursed, huh?"

"Hell yeah. Told me I gotta do what's right and being with you is what feels right to me."

"Being with you feels right. I need to know more, Hans."

"What you talking about?"

"Why'd you up and leave and not tell anyone? How did you get shot."

He sighed, leaned back and finished the rest of his drink. From the change in his body language, I could tell he didn't feel like having this conversation. "I don't want to talk about this right now."

"We should talk about it right now. You're coming into my life after being gone for years. I want to know why."

"I was shot because niggas didn't want to see me do great shit in the hood. Jealousy was the reason I took a bullet to the back."

"I know you. You don't run from a fight. Why did you disappear like you never existed?"

"Haze. If it was just me, I would have tried to take a nigga's head off. Even with me being in the position I was in. Haze needed me, and I didn't want to bury my brother because of my ego."

"Understandable."

"You done with your questions?"

"Who shot you."

"Bridge."

I gasped when he said it. When I first heard about what happened with Hans I had reached out to him and never got a response back. Never did I expect Bridge to have anything to do with him being shot.

"Why?"

"Because he couldn't take that I could run New York better than he did. His connect wanted me to take over New York."

"Bridge *is* the connect."

He chuckled. "You worked with him that long and don't know he has a connect. Bridge is a small fish compared to who is on top of him," he popped a piece of steak into his mouth. "The nigga is just the face."

"Wow," I was shocked because as much as I've worked for Bridge, I never knew he worked with a connect. He always made it seem like he was the connect and that's how he got shipments in the way he did. All this time that slimy nigga had been working for someone else. It all made sense. I didn't understand how he took such a hearty cut from us. His ass was taking his cut, and the cut to pay off his fucking supplier.

"Yeah. He tried to have me killed. I don't think he knows that I'm alive."

"You've never thought about getting even with him?"

"Yeah, it's crossed my mind recently."

"Recently?"

"Yeah."

"Why recently?"

"Kenni."

"What about Kenni?"

"She can tell me where that nigga be. That's if I ever wanted to get back at him," he shrugged.

"How do you know she would do that?" I wanted Bridge dead more than anything. I've always dreamed about killing that nigga my damn self. The way he treated Kenni and put his hands on her further added to my anger.

"I don't know that. It doesn't hurt to ask her."

"Kenni is stupid over him."

"Kenni didn't have Haze in her life." He brought up a valid reason. Kenni had been reaching out to me more and all she spoke about was Haze.

She had been all smiles whenever she spoke about Haze. I was happy that he made her that happy. If she'd listened to me, she could have always been happy.

"You're right."

"I didn't bring you out to talk about this nigga. I wanted to spend time with you, and you only." He kissed the back of my hand.

"We'll revisit this topic again."

"Bet." He stood up and came around the table to kiss me on the lips. This feeling felt like someone was going to pinch and wake me up any minute.

Eleven

Brix

WHEN SAYLOR CALLED and told me that she wanted to meet at the soul food restaurant we first bumped into each other, I was about to run out the crib that night to meet her. She told me she was coming to Maryland for the day and wanted to talk to me. Shit had been tense around the house. Juleena was growing tired of her recovery. While we all thought she was recovering well, she was upset because she wasn't recovering fast enough. She was lucky to be alive and here she was complaining about not recovering fast enough. I knew why she wanted to be recovered. Her ass wanted to follow me around and see what the fuck I was up to. Sitting in the house all day was boring and she wanted to see where I was going. All I did was make sure she was straight, food runs and picking the kids up from school. When Jessica came over, then I used that as my time to handle business and touch bases with Bridge. Me and him were on different pages lately. He was so consumed with his own life that he was letting shit basically run itself. Each time I tried to get with him or Supreme about it, they told me not to worry about it. Saylor warned me a while ago that they still saw me as the little nigga. When she said that shit, I told her she was bugging and that Bridge knew how much work I put in. Now sitting back, I was his little errand boy. When he needed me to sit and watch someone, I was the man.

"Why are you going out again? You just came back. Nobody is here with me." Juleena wheeled behind me into the kitchen.

"Babe, I'll be gone for two hours at the most. I put your lunch in the fridge and everything you need is right at your fingertips. Your mom said she'll pop in after her nail appointment," I told her.

"I don't like being home alone like this, Brix. You know I get anxiety and start panicking," I sighed and sat down at the table.

"Juleena, you're a grown woman. I'm not going to put off things I need to do because you want me to sit in the house with you. You're healed enough to transfer yourself on and off the couch."

Juleena was playing that role all too well. She wanted to be helpless when it was convenient for her. All she did was sit on the couch with her laptop and order shit. She went as far as to get a queen size bed for the guest room downstairs so I could sleep downstairs with her. Somehow every morning she found her way to the bottom of the bed to wake me up with head, yet she couldn't sit home for a few hours alone? This was the shit that pissed me off about her. We were back fucking and she always wanted the dick. I'm not going to front, I wanted to give it to her. Fucking her seemed to keep her quiet and content. She didn't nag and was happy that I was giving her dick normally again.

Here. I got the message from Saylor.

"Whatever. Always putting business before me."

"I'm not doing this with you, Juleena," I told her and kissed her on the forehead. She watched me leave the house.

Jumping into my car, I sped to the diner. It was fifteen minutes from my crib. Thinking about Juleena, I was pissed. She always pulled this shit. It seemed like she wanted me to herself. I just needed to breathe. All I wanted was to have healthy space from each other. Once we got together it was like she stopped hanging around her friends. She put her all into what we had and that seemed to be her friend, hobby and life. So, when I wanted to chill with my niggas or do something alone she acted like I was doing something wrong. Couples needed their own outlet and alone time, but Juleena didn't understand that shit. I found parking out front of the diner and headed inside. Saylor was waiting at the table with a glass of sweet tea.

"My bad. I had to make sure Juleena was good before I left the house," I walked over to her side and hugged her.

Something about her appeared different to me. "It's cool."

"So, what's up?"

She laughed. "You don't want to go up and order your food?"

"Nah, I'm not hungry."

"Brix, go and order your food. What's the rush? Let's have lunch together." She told me, so I went and ordered food.

I got my usual when I came here. Meatloaf, mash potatoes and mac and cheese. They handed me my ticket to put on the table so they could bring the food to the table. When I got back to the table she was just wrapping up a conversation on the phone.

"Talk to you soon," she said before ending her call. "I'm starving. Sitting in that prison for four hours without eating with Darren is horrible."

She had told me about she and Darren keeping in touch and how she put money on his books. I thought she was solid for that. Bridge's ass didn't even reach out to him. It was like Darren never existed in his life. The only time he brought him up was to use him as a lesson how not to be.

"Oh word. You went to see him?"

"Yeah. He asked me to come see him. I didn't like how he sounded so I made a quick trip here to visit him."

"He good in there?"

"Nah. They added an additional fifteen years onto his sentence."

"Fuck. Why?"

"He was caught with a shank, and one of the prisoners had just been stabbed in the back in the shower... turns out Darren did it."

"The fuck he in there stabbing people for? He supposed to do his time and get the fuck outta there."

"Same thing I told him. His wife served him with divorce papers and she's moving the kids to Missouri."

"Word?" I didn't see Darren's wife around like that, and I hadn't kept in contact because me and Darren weren't that close. I wondered if Bridge helped her out with money because Darren was locked up. Knowing him, he probably acted like he didn't know her ass either.

"Yep. She got her a new man in the army. He wants to move her and the kids in his house and marry her. Darren gave her his blessings to go."

"He act like he had a choice."

Saylor laughed. "Right. He still thinks he running shit in there. Let him tell it, he the man up in that place."

"Reason why his ass doing an additional fifteen years."

"Yep. He talking about he want to be with me and want me to wait for him. I told his ass that I could hold him down for the rest of the year, but he's going to have to get a pen pal."

"You dead wrong."

"Shit, what I look like? He's a bill. He can write me and I'll be there as a friend, but I can't be paying all the money I do for his books. Plus, I'm not about to be with him for fifteen additional years. I got a life too," she rolled her eyes.

"I feel you," I chuckled.

The lady from the front came and put our food down onto the table. She took my drink order and went to fulfill it. "I'm glad that we could have lunch together."

"Yeah, me too. We need to do this more often."

I didn't like the look of her face when I said that. "What's been going on with you?"

"Trying to find the balance with everything going on."

"Still? It's been at least a month and then some since the accident." She looked surprised to see that I was still going through all of this with Juleena. Hell, I was surprised that I was even going through all this with Juleena.

"Yeah, she's been healing good. Just gotta take it slow."

"I'm glad she's doing better."

"What's good with us? I hit you up and you take hours to reply, or don't reply at all. I haven't spoken to you in a week, then you randomly want to have lunch with me."

She took a bite out of her chicken. "I can't see you anymore. I'm in a relationship and it's disrespectful to my man." She revealed. I felt like I had been punched in the throat when the words left her lips.

"What you mean? I thought we were doing something."

"Brix, we weren't doing nothing. Other than the same thing we were doing back then. Me hiding and having half of you, and I'm not willing to do that. I want to be happy and in love with a man that's mine, not sharing you with Juleena."

"I'll leave her."

"No you won't. You're in too deep. Y'all live together and you help raise her kids. Who are you kidding?"

It wouldn't be easy to leave Juleena, but I would do it for Saylor. Having her come back into my life relit something inside of me. I wanted to be with her and show her that I loved her more than she knew, and how the decision I made back then was the wrong one. I wanted, nah I needed Saylor.

"Baby, I promise if you give me time that I will end things with her."

"Time? I can't give you time, Brix. You've had all this time to choose what you wanted and you stayed with her. Instead, you continued to build with her. I'm not telling you to leave her because of me. I'm happy and for the first time I see this going somewhere and don't want to fuck it up."

"Damn, Saylor."

"I'm sorry, but I felt like it was better to meet here. It's always going to be her, and you're always going to run for her and those boys. I don't knock it, but I know that us trying to rekindle whatever we had isn't going to work."

"Have you even tried? I've been trying to link with you and show you that I love you and want to make you happy, and you've been playing me off."

"I've been playing you off because I know this is a

dangerous game and I'll be the one getting hurt. Juleena isn't willing to let you go."

"You don't know that. Ma, let me make you happy," I was damn near pleading with her. We didn't bump into each other by mistake. This was supposed to happen. "Fate brought us here."

"No, my hungry ass brought me here... you have a trap not too far from here. It wasn't fate. It was the fact that you happened to be hungry that day. You're always going to choose her and that's something I've made peace with. I got a man that's going to always put me first for once. It's time for me to be happy, Brix." She softened her voice.

I looked down at my phone because it had been going off in my pocket. When I looked down at my phone it was Jessica calling me. "I gotta take this," I told her and answered.

Saylor shrugged and continued to eat her food. "Do you."

"Jessica, what's up?"

"I just came over after my nail appointment and Juleena was laid out on the floor in front of the fridge. When I came in, she was trying to reach her cellphone to call you. I'm going to bring her to the emergency room to make sure everything is alright with her," she informed me.

"Shit."

"Meet us at the emergency room when you can," she said before ending the call.

Saylor just sat here and told me that Juleena would always come first, and I pleaded and told her that I would leave her. Now, I had to run to be by her side because she fell in the kitchen. It hurt because I really wanted to be with Saylor, but it was like I couldn't because of everything I had built with Juleena. Me leaving her meant that I had to leave her kids. And, at times they were hard headed and spoiled, but that didn't mean that I didn't care about them. Even though I was never in love with Juleena, I had love for her and cared about how things would end between us.

Saylor was enjoying her food when I ended the call. "Everything good?"

"Nah Juleena fell and she's on her way to the hospital," I said, biting the shit out of my lip.

"I know you have to go."

"I do. I wanna continue to have this conversation with you. Give me like an hour and I'll link back with you."

She sighed. "Brix, it's over. You have too much going on right now, and people that need you. Go and be with her, she needs you." Her hand laid on top of mine. Just feeling her touch made me want to fuck everything and be with her.

"Nah, Saylor…. We gotta finish this conversation."

She was quiet for a minute, then sighed. "Okay."

I grabbed my phone, kissed her on the forehead and headed to the door. When I got outside, I looked inside and saw her grab her phone and smile when she spoke to whoever was on the phone. The sad thing was, I knew that this would probably be the last time that I would see Saylor again.

When I got to the hospital, Juleena had already been checked out by the doctor and was ready to be discharged. I wanted to talk to the doctor myself so we sat around waiting for him. She had an attitude because I left her and she fell. Part of me felt like she had thrown herself on the floor to prove to me that she couldn't be left alone. I wasn't stupid. Juleena had never fell before, so why now did she fall? Especially trying to get something out the fridge. I put everything she needed on the counter where she could reach.

"Why were you in the fridge in the first place?" I broke the silence in the room. Jessica was reading on her kindle, and Juleena was texting on her phone.

"Is that what you're going to ask? I can't believe you." She sucked her teeth and turned her back to me.

"You ain't answer the question."

"I wanted to get me a cold drink. I'm tired of drinking hot ass soda because that's the only thing that I can reach." She replied. "I would have had it, if the fridge door didn't hit the wheel chair."

"Her physical therapy starts next week. Thank God. I know you're tired of being in that chair, baby," Jessica said, not bothering to look up from her kindle.

"I am. I want to be independent again. I'm tired of depending on everybody and feeling like I'm a burden."

"Nobody ever said you were a burden, Juleena. You act like I'm supposed to sit in the house with you all day. I gotta make money and can't afford to sit there all day," I never wanted to tell her, but money was tight as fuck.

With the dumb ass moves that Bridge was doing, money wasn't the same. He seemed to be the only one fucking eating. With the increase in his cut, it was hard to turn a profit. I had savings that I've been holding onto, because this street shit wasn't forever. Still, my main money was running low and I had bills that had to be paid.

"Hi, I was told that you wanted to speak with me?"

"Yes. I'm her boyfriend," I stood up and shook the doctor's hand. "Brix."

"Well, Mr. Brix... she fell, but she's going to be just fine. She informed me of her back surgery and I checked there.

Nothing is out of the norm, however I told her that her that she might feel some soreness on her body tomorrow morning. The baby wasn't hurt either," he explained.

"Wait a minute... rewind that... baby?"

"Yes. She's pregnant. It was a surprise for her too," he smiled. "Congratulations."

"Damn." Was all I muttered.

"Here's her discharge papers. I want her to check with her primary doctor in a few days to make sure everything is still alright. In the future, please be very careful. You're carrying precious cargo." He winked, handed me the discharge papers and left the room.

"Why didn't you tell me that you were pregnant?" I needed to sit down. The room felt like it was spinning around.

"Because I didn't know, Brix. It was a surprise to me too."

"This baby is a blessing and a second chance... I know you have her now. I'll go pick the boys up from school." Jessica kissed Juleena, then me on the cheek before she left.

Juleena rubbed her stomach and looked at me. "This baby means a lot to me. Even if you don't want it, I want my baby," she looked me in the eyes.

"I never said I didn't want a baby. Right now isn't the time."

"Brix, we've been fucking raw... if you didn't want a baby then you should have strapped up."

"Please. If I strapped up you would have been in your feelings about the shit."

"So, I basically made you give me a baby? I made you nut inside of me? Typical you shit." She rolled her eyes at me.

"I'm not saying that, Ju."

"I didn't say nothing when I almost lost my life following

behind your ass. You and Saylor been meeting up and you want to know why I want your ass back home."

Shit. I knew there was another reason for her being in Virginia when she was in the accident. That lie she told everyone was bullshit. I had been too caught up in other shit to be worried about that.

"She's getting back in the game. We met up to talk about what needs to be done," I lied.

"How about I call Bridge and ask him," she threatened.

I couldn't let her see me sweat. "Go ahead."

"Is that all your meeting was about?"

"Yeah. Why would we be together all this time for me to go and be with someone else? We got a baby on the way and don't need to be doing all this stressing and shit."

A nigga wanted to cry. A baby? With a baby I would never be able to get away from Juleena. She would always be a part of my life. She grabbed my hand and put it on her stomach. There was nothing there and it was typical extra Juleena.

"We made this blessing." She looked at me. "Whatever you and Saylor have going on, you need to end it. I don't believe that shit about work. She would meet with Bridge before you." She tightly gripped my hand. "I'm not happy and it's going to take a lot for me to trust you, but we can work through it."

I just nodded my head because I knew that there was no way I would be able to get away from Juleena. At least, by not hurting her. I had a seed on the way so my focus was on making sure that my seed was brought into this world healthy. If I had to play my part to make sure my kid was straight, that was what I had to do.

"Yeah. We'll make it work," I squeezed her hand and kissed her on the lips. In the back of my head, I was thinking about Saylor.

Twelve

Hans

I WAS BACK in Virginia for a few days to handle business. Both my brothers acted like I had been gone for a year with the way they both were blowing my phone up. Saylor had some meetings back in New York. She was in the process of starting a house cleaning company. I admired how she was in the game and got out and had all these businesses. She kept telling me that I needed to get out and do something legit. I think she told me more out of fear. More than anybody, Saylor knew exactly how ruthless the game was. She knew that I could be here today and gone tomorrow because some nigga was jealous of what I had worked hard for. I understood what she was saying and I had some businesses in the works. As far as the game, I had no plans on stepping back.

"About time you're home. I came by here and your ass was

gone. When were you going to tell me that you went back to New York?" Kook walked into my condo.

"It was something last minute," I grabbed a bottle of orange juice out the fridge. Being back in my condo felt good. It had been a minute since I had checked in. The cleaning lady I hired made sure my shit stayed clean and stocked with whatever I needed.

"To go and be with shorty?" he raised his eyebrow. "Y'all together or something? You don't never travel for no pussy."

"Yeah. We made it official."

"Shit, you and Saylor finally got that shit right," Haze walked into the door next. "Kook, next time you see a nigga lightly jogging and saying hold the elevator, hold that shit." He mushed our brother.

"Oh shit, that was you? Thought that was some Indian nigga... you know you look a little Indian."

"Fuck you." Haze dapped me up and took a seat at the counter. "Good to see you back in the city," he joked.

"Y'all acting like I been gone for long."

"A whole month, Hans. You been in New York for a fucking month."

"And? Shit was handled."

"Yeah. It was." Haze laughed. "I'm glad that you both got your shit right... So you 'bout to move back home?"

"We not even talking about that right now. I spend time in New York and she'll spend time here in Virginia. I'm not trying to make shit complicated. We both know what we want, and that's all we're focused on."

"I hear that." Haze agreed.

"What's good with the both of you?"

"Meeka had a miscarriage," Kook revealed. "She been real

depressed and shit, so that's why I haven't been around. Trying to make sure my baby is straight... feel me?"

"Damn... tell sis that I'm sorry."

"Me too," I added.

Kook was a fool, demanding and wanted shit how he wanted. However, there was no denying how much he loved him some Meeka and their daughter. "I will. She went to the spa with her cousins, so I'm just chilling right now."

"You a good ass nigga," Haze slapped him on the back. "You really are."

"Appreciate that."

"Me and Whiney haven't been on the same page. She been hanging out with her cousins in Philly."

"Isn't she the same bitch that gets mad when you go and grab a burger from the other side of town without telling her?" I asked.

"Yeah. She don't see why I have a problem with it."

Kook laughed. "Yo, you don't sound like a nigga that's really bothered. If Meeka was hanging out in Philly, I'm gonna be in the fucking trunk of her whip."

"You crazy as shit," I laughed. "But, Kook got a point. You don't sound bothered."

"Me and Kenni been kicking it like crazy." Just the look of his face when he mentioned Kenni's name told me that this nigga was all smitten and shit.

"Look at you blushing like a little bitch. She make you that happy?"

"Hell yeah. She changed... she's not that same Kenni that I was telling you about," he told Kook.

"Shit, Meeka told me how she used to be. I was wondering why you were even wasting your time trying to kick it with her again."

"Nah, she definitely changed. She had time to mature," I spoke up.

Kenni was like a little sister to me. She was always about money, clothes and what a nigga could offer her. Being around her recently, I could tell that she was different. Time had passed and she had matured and realized that money wasn't everything.

"You hit that yet?"

"Nah. That's not what I'm worried about," Haze replied.

"He trying to be one of those niggas that takes his time... I see you." Kook nudged him with his shoulder.

We all laughed. "On the real, I want her in the worse way possible. She told me how that pussy ass nigga be beating on her," he revealed.

Me and Haze hadn't sat down and spoke about him and Kenni much. I knew he was hanging out with her because of Saylor. Last we spoke about Bridge was when we were all at the trap house.

"When I worked for his ass, he was fucking up the hoes he used to fuck. Those bitches would come back after he blackened their eye or busted their lip."

This abuse shit wasn't something new to Bridge. If I didn't have my own shit going on I could have warned Kenni. Crazy thing, if I did warn her, she wouldn't have listened. Bridge was showing her something that she had never had; love. He was buying her whatever she wanted and introducing her to a new life that she had been trying to get since she hit puberty. If I tried to look out, she would have told me I was being a hater and did her own thing anyway. Sometimes, you had to let people learn on their own.

"And she still with him? The fuck is she with him for?"

Kook wondered. "Let me hit Meeka, she'd be gone with my daughter."

"Some women aren't like that... Kenni probably feel like she needs this nigga," I voiced. "He took her out the hood and introduced her to a better life. She didn't have much family like that before, but I know he made it seem like he was all she had."

"Terri is dying. She has liver failure," Haze revealed. He told us how they had met up last month and got into an argument, which lead to him going to her hotel room.

"Damn. Terri used to drink like a fish and smoke like a damn pipe," I sighed. "She and her mother been good?"

"Nah, she haven't spoke to her in years. She got in contact with Esma and wants to see Kenni. She been going back and forth on if she wants to visit her."

"She and Terri had a bad ass relationship. Terri used to treat her like she was a roommate... you could hear her tearing into Kenni from in front of the building."

"Can you blame shorty for trying to claw her way out the hood? With a mama like that, I would have been trying to get the fuck away too." Kook grabbed a banana from the fruit bowl on the counter.

"Remember what we were talking about?"

"We talk about a lot of shit... nigga jog my memory," I laughed and took a sip of my orange juice.

"About setting Bridge up."

"Oh, now this nigga wanna do it." Kook laughed.

"I don't want to include Kenni in this shit. He'll fucking kill her if he found out." He warned both of us. "This is between us."

"How the fuck you think we're going to get information on this nigga?" Kook asked.

"Saylor," I replied.

"You pillow talking already, nigga?" Haze looked at me.

I laughed. "She worked with Bridge's ass for years... she knows the nigga better than we do. She can't stand his ass either."

"Just because she can't stand him doesn't mean she's willing to set him up. Shorty gotta have some type of loyalty to him." Kook said.

"Not when the nigga is beating on her best friend. Saylor can't stand that nigga and that's the main reason for getting out the game... she couldn't work for him no more," I further explained everything that Saylor had explained to me.

One night we sat up talking and she spoke about how she would have probably been in the drug game if it wasn't for Bridge. The disgust that laced her tongue when she spoke of this nigga told me that she hated him. Everything about him she hated, including that Kenni was even with him.

"Ight. So we doing this? I want that nigga dead." Haze looked me in the eyes. I could tell he was serious about this shit.

"What are you looking to accomplish with killing this nigga? Getting the girl?"

"Nah. I want her to be happy, even if it's not with me. Long as he still breathing she's not going to leave him."

"Shouldn't that be left up to her. I get being abused and shit, but she keep going back or better yet, she not leaving. Killing him isn't going to do shit but have her find the next nigga to take care of her."

"On the real, Kook. She not even like that. When we were younger, maybe. Now, I can tell she wanna get the fuck away from this nigga, but he's never going to leave her alone."

"I'm down for anything." Kook shrugged his shoulders.

"Whatever you're wanting to do, I'm down... I'll let Saylor

know too," I told Haze. He was serious about Kenni, so I wanted to help in any way that I could. "You know that nigga had it coming anyway."

"Bet," Haze said.

"As far as everything, we good and everything running smooth?" I asked them. Since Kook been dealing with Meeka, I knew it was Haze making sure everything was good.

"Hell yeah. We're good," Haze replied.

"The only reason this nigga is asking because he about to head back to New York." Kook laughed.

"Fuck you," I continued to laugh.

I never realized how much that I missed home until I was back there. There was no city that compared to growing up in New York city. Us, New Yorkers just had a different hustle than the rest of the county. I loved being able to leave Saylor's crib and drive to the hood and get food from a corner store. In Virginia, the shit wasn't the same. It had me thinking about what Kook had been trying to do all along. Maybe starting shit in New York wasn't a bad thing after all. I knew Bridge wasn't moving work out there since Darren had got knocked. He stuck to his original places.

"We don't wanna hold your stank ass up. Go back to your girl," Haze joked.

"On the real, I might be taking a trip out the country," I warned them both.

They both looked at me. "I want to take Saylor to Thailand. I saw her watching some documentary about the country and she mentioned she wanted to visit it one day. Plus, I want her to try real Thai food, since that's all she eats."

"You bout to spend a bag on taking her out the country to try some authentic Thai food. Haze, you remember when I took Meeka to Jamaica and this nigga called me a soft cornball?"

"I sure as fuck do remember. Kook, you remember when I took Whitney to Canada and he called me a wannabe Drake ass nigga?"

"I had to agree with him... the fuck is in Canada?"

I laughed so hard I had to lean over the sink to avoid spitting juice in their face. "A lot of shit. She wanted to go there... fuck you."

"Bruh, Whitney is weird as fuck. She picked there out of all places," I continued to laugh. "I hear what y'all saying. I gave y'all shit for doing shit for your girls."

"Did you? Nigga, every time you said something it was about us going on trips with our girl. Now you think we about to let you go easy? Hell nah." Kook laughed.

"Despite you being a dick... I think that shit is dope and she'll enjoy it," Haze told me. "Don't get used to leaving the country like that. You still got shit here too."

"I hear you; I hear you," I laughed. We sat talking and catching up like we usually did. I didn't realize I missed my brothers as much as I did. It was like I had to split my time between here and New York. I loved being under Saylor and spending time with her. We had got into our own routine and shit. When she wanted her space, I gave it to her and she did the same with me. I ran by my house before getting on the road back to New York.

When I pulled into the driveway, all the lights were off. It was a little after two in the morning. Before leaving, I ended up stopping by Haze's to chat with him alone. We always had conversations with just the two of us. Before Kook came into the picture, it was just the two of us. After he gave me his official blessings with me and Saylor, I got on the highway to come back to New York. Using Saylor's key, I let myself back in and put my suitcase to the right of the foyer. Kicking my sneakers off, I made my way upstairs to Saylor's room. The light from the TV flashed from under the door. She always slept with the TV on whenever she slept alone. When I was with her, she turned the TV off and stayed snuggled up to me. Opening the door, I closed it behind me and quickly got undressed and climbed into bed.

While I was kicking it with Haze, I was busy making arrangements to take her out the country and she didn't even know it. "Baby, you're back?" she said sleepily.

"Yeah. I'm back," I kissed her on the lips and moved closer to her. "Ma, I need you to pack in the morning, alright?"

She yawned. "Pack? Pack for what?" she put her ice cold feet on my leg, like she always did.

"I'm taking you on a trip."

"What about Nana? I can't leave her again." She spoke with her eyes closed. I knew she was tired and would probably ask me if she was dreaming in the morning.

"She coming too. You gotta tell her to pack too," I told her.

"K." A few seconds later, she was lightly snoring on my chest. I watched the reruns of Seinfeld for a bit before dozing off to sleep with her in my arms.

Saylor slept peacefully on the bed while I opened up the sliding doors and looked out at the water from our waterfront suite. We had our own balcony with a pool on it. I surprised Saylor with a trip to Thailand. She never asked for anything, and because of that I wanted to give her everything. The whole time I had her and Esma packing, they both kept asking where we were going. I called my nigga up and he loaned us his jet for the trip. She had no idea where we were going until we landed and had to get our passports stamped and go through customs. They were both shocked and happy. Seeing how happy it made them made me happier. Esma was as close as a mother that I could have. Seeing her excited about getting out the country was all that I needed. I promised her that I would make Saylor happy and wouldn't hurt her, and I planned to keep my word. Saylor meant so much to me that I wanted to spend all my time making her happy. I never had the reason to travel the world. I always called my brothers soft for traveling the world with their women. Now, I was a soft ass nigga because Saylor made me want to do all those things. It was easy to be so knee deep in the game that you didn't take time to live.

Since me and Haze left New York, all my time went into making sure we never had to starve again. I wanted to make sure that we were good for life. Even with Haze being grown and capable of taking care of himself, I still wanted to make sure my brother was good. I realized that I never took time for me or trying to find love. I've had small ass relationships, but never taking them serious because of the streets. I was so consumed with making money that my personal life suffered. I never realized how much I needed love until Saylor came back into my life. That was when I realized that God was giving me a sign. He was telling me to slow down and smell the roses. He put Saylor back in my path for a reason and I'd be damn if I fucked it up with her.

"That bird been chirping since before the sun rose," Saylor wrapped her arms around my waist and reached up to kiss me on the shoulder. "Why are you awake so early?"

"I wanted to catch the sun rise," I pulled her around and held her into my arms. "You slept good?"

"I can't believe that we're in Thailand. Kenni is so jealous," she laughed. "Why are we here?"

"I want to travel the world with you and Nana," I smirked. Esma had her own suite right next to ours.

"I love how you care for me and her... like we're a package deal."

"That's because you are. Esma has always been there for me and my brothers. Yeah, I cut her out of my life a lot as we got older, but that never stopped her from making sure we were good," I kissed her on the lips.

"She's always been like that."

"I know, and that's how she raised an incredible woman. Saylor, I wanna love you until the day that I die. I wanna experience everything with you." She kissed me on the lips.

"Hans, I wanna do that and then more with you. These past few months have been amazing. You've shown me that love is real, and that it's not something that I should have to fight for. Because of you, I don't always have to keep that hard wall up and pretend to be so hard... I can be real with you, a woman." She hugged me.

"I love you, Saylor."

"I love you too." we both kissed each other and held onto each other. "With you, I feel like you're not going to break my heart. I want to have a future and a family with you, Hans."

I picked her up and kissed her on the lips. "How about you come and show me in the bed?" I kissed her again on the lips.

"Um, I'm ovulating right now." She looked away.

"Oh word? Even more reason why you need to come and show me," I nibbled on her earlobe.

"You trying to knock me up, huh?"

"Hell yeah... I've waited a long time for this.. I'm not about to waste any more time," I carried her into the room and shut the patio door.

I wanted everything that came with love. The babies, marriage and the big picket fenced house. Shit, I'd even take the dog too. Nah, I should say. I wanted everything that came with Saylor. We both waited for this and now it was happening. We both deserved happiness.

Bridge

KENNI HAD BEEN ACTING REAL different lately. She had been happy and I know I wasn't the nigga making her happy, so who the fuck was it. The way she dressed up told me that it had to be another nigga. She was wearing makeup more often, getting her hair done and all that other shit. Even when I told her I was dipping out; she didn't trip how she used to. I know Jahiem told us niggas to put that woman first, but I had too many damn women around me. Mercedes could possibly be pregnant. She was waiting for her period, and I knew that we had planned for this. Then, India, she been on some shit where she didn't let me see the kids. I called and she would hang up. When I popped up to the crib, she had the locks changed. Then, Kenni. She seemed to be the easiest to deal with. Her ass was home with a smile and making sure everything was how it was supposed to be.

"Where you going?" I asked, when she strutted past me in the den. She turned and looked at me, not a look that said *I loved my nigga*, but one that said *this nigga getting on my nerves.*

"I'm driving into New York to see my mother. Saylor said that I could stay with her for a few days."

"Your moms? You think I'm stupid? You and Terri haven't spoken in years," I caught her dumb ass in her lie.

"I told you she wanted to see me... she's dying, Maurice." She tried to jog my memory. I remember her telling me something about her mother, but I was too in my feelings about India's ass changing the locks on me. It had been at least a month and some change since I saw my son and daughter.

"I remember."

"Yeah. So, I'll see you in a few days."

"Fuck you gotta stay with Saylor for? Bring your ass right back home soon as you finish," I told her. She thought she was slick by trying to stay in New York.

"I don't want to drive at night... Me and Saylor were going to hang too," she tried to explain.

"Matter fact, I'm going to come so you don't have to drive there or back," I told her.

"Maurice, I'm an adult. You don't need to come with me everywhere." She walked closer to me. "A few days apart from each other isn't going to hurt." She kissed me on the cheek.

"Ight. I guess you can go there by yourself," I sighed.

"Thanks, babe. I call you when I get there," she told me and then rushed out the house before I could even say another word.

The reason I decided not to go was because I had to go see my other daughter. Misa, was the chick that had the baby at the mall. Kenni's ass was so nosey and always trying to find a nigga cheating. Misa played her part well, which is why I put her up in a nice ass condo not too far from my crib. She was living in the hood when I met her at a strip club one night. She was out with her girls and I was there with a few of my niggas. She was the prettiest thing walking in that bitch. We exchanged numbers and linked a few times. She was one of those good bitches that didn't let you hit on the first night. I bought her a few bags and shit, and that's when the legs opened for me. She found out that she was pregnant and kept the shit from me. When I found out from her big mouth friend, I popped up at her crib. She kept the pregnancy from me because she didn't want me to think that I trapped her. That shit spoke to me and I told her that long as she got my seed, I was going to take care of her.

Kenni swore she knew everything and that's why her ass was being so nosey in the mall. Her ass should have been happy that we were out shopping, but she had to ruin shit. Misa wasn't into the drama. She knew about Kenni and told me that she didn't need that drama. India and Mercedes knew nothing about her. I wanted to keep that shit like that. Misa was a good one and didn't nag me. She never called me and begged me to come spend time with our daughter. Whenever I showed up was good enough with her. Mercedes and India's ass was good for calling and causing an argument between me and Kenni. Misa was different. She was in dental school and her mother watched our daughter. For her birthday I had bought her a brand-new car. She was grateful for all the shit I did for her, so she didn't need to start no drama. When Kia was born, I knew that little girl was mine. She looked just like Mia. I was the one who came up with the name Kia.

I grabbed the phone and called Mercedes. She had been hitting me up since last night. I had to fight with Kenni to get some pussy and head last night, so I wasn't about to stop for nobody. The way my baby sucked my dick was like an art. Her ass needed to be teaching a class or something. Usually when we fucked, she would be wet as a fucking ocean. Her shit was dry and her moans kept sounding forced as fuck. I've been busting up in her and she hadn't gotten pregnant yet. I knew soon that we were going to a doctor's appointment because something had to be wrong. I had been busting babies up in everybody else, and the one person I wanted to carry my seed wasn't getting pregnant.

"Hey," Mercedes's voice came through the line.

"You called last night, what's up?"

She sighed. "I wanted some dick. You've been real distant since we got back from Miami and I let it rock because you needed to spend time with your girl, but damn... I want some of you too."

This was the problem with Mercedes. She thought she was more than a baby mama. I was probably to blame too. I allowed her to feel like she was more than a baby mother. Taking her and our daughter on trips, letting her talk me into another baby and doing all the shit I knew I shouldn't have been doing.

"I already told you about calling me at night. Kenni be bugging about that shit, and that shit cause problems in my home."

"And how is she going to feel when this new baby is coming?"

"So the blood test came back?"

"Yep. I told you that I'm fertile as hell." She laughed.

"She not going to find out about this new baby. I don't give a fuck who you gotta say is your baby daddy. Kenni would lose her shit if she found out about this new baby."

"Keep dicking me down like you've promised and that won't be a problem."

I looked at the phone and then put it back to my ear. "You threatening me, Mercedes?"

"Take it however you want. I refuse for me and my children

to be neglected because you're trying to get in good with Kenni." She ended the call.

Instead of calling her back and threatening to kick her ass down the stairs, I went and got showered to head over to Misa's crib. She was the peace when my life was a storm. Misa never added to any of my problems. It didn't take me long to make it to her condo. Using my key, I entered the crib. She was at the kitchen table studying and our daughter was asleep in her bouncer.

"Hey Bridge... you didn't tell me you were coming over," she smiled when she saw me. Closing her laptop, she walked over to me and kissed me on the lips.

"Oh my bad. I gotta tell you when I'm coming to see you and my seed?"

She laughed. "No, but you should have told me so I could have warmed some food up for you." That was another thing about Misa. The bitch loved to cook and was good at that shit. She made that kind of food that made your toes curl when you tasted it.

"It's all good. I'm about to put some basketball shorts on and watch the news," I told her. When Misa moved in, I put some clothes in the his and hers closet in the master bedroom. Whenever I laid low, I was always here. Nobody knew about her and I wanted to keep it like that. She would cook, clean, fuck, and suck my dick all while taking care of our daughter.

"Alright. Let me put Kia down in her nursery and then I'll warm the food up," she told me.

I walked over and looked at my beautiful ass daughter. Between her, Mia, and Mya, I was going to have to keep my gun on me at all times. My daughters were beautiful as shit. I wanted Mercedes to have another girl, because Kenni was going to have my next son. It had been something I was speaking on and had faith that it was going to happen – soon.

"She getting so damn big."

"Kia mama is a greedy butt," she kissed her on the cheek and patted her butt. "Wanna hold her?"

"Yeah," I gently took her and kissed her on the lips. "Pretty ass," I walked upstairs and put her in the bed, while I changed. When I was done, I got into the bed and turned on the TV.

"Awe, my babies," Misa smiled when she saw us in the bed. "I'm jealous because I have to study for this test tomorrow."

"You've studied enough. Come lay down with me and the baby," I told her.

She nodded her head and left the room. When she came back, she had a plate of food and climbed into the bed with me. "Damn, you cooked all this yesterday?"

"Yeah... My mama came over with my little cousins and we all ate," she explained. Misa's mama had been wanting to meet me for a while. I didn't want to meet her because I didn't feel like answering questions about our future. Right now we were cool. We didn't need to add anything extra to the shit. All that pressure was what fucked up relationships.

"Oh word?" I shoved some chicken into my mouth.

"Mama still wants to meet you." She reminded me like she always did whenever she mentioned her mother.

"And I told you that I don't need to meet her right now. All she needs to know is that Kia's father is providing for the both of you."

"I know, I tell her every time. It still doesn't stop her from asking about you. My family is curious how I afford a place out here and a new car."

"Tell them that you got a baby father that makes shit

happen for you," I replied while shoving more food into my mouth.

I couldn't remember the last time Kenni made some shit that was good. Lately, she been putting some bullshit together and calling it dinner. When she first moved to Maryland, she used to cook her ass off. Now, I didn't even want the shit she made. Come to think about it, her ass wasn't even eating the food she was cooking. She kept telling me she found the recipe online. Her ass needed to keep them shits online.

"I appreciate you, baby," she reached over and kissed me on the lips. "I'm going to put Kia in her bed so she can get some sleep," she told me and left the room.

I had finished my food and when she came back, I was in the middle of the bed stroking my dick. Misa already knew what time it was. She undressed and climbed on the bed from the bottom. She took my dick into her mouth and down her throat. She twirled her tongue around my dick while it was down her throat. She hummed and massaged my balls at the same time. She had my eyes damn near in the back of my head. When she pulled my dick out of her mouth, she spit on it a few times before swallowing that shit whole again. She held my dick at the shaft, popped it out of her mouth and nibbled at the tip of my dick. Shit, all ladies needed to do this shit. Her bites weren't hard, soft nibbles at the tip of my dick while she applied pressure to the shaft of my dick. Just when I was about to explode, she lowered that pussy right on it and held onto the headboard and rocked my fucking world. If she would have asked who was daddy, my ass probably would have said her. I held onto her hips and let her finish taking me on a ride. When I came, I held her hips and she came right along with me. We collapsed on the bed and was soon knocked out with the TV as background noise.

☆

My phone started ringing and woke me up from my sleep. When I came over here, it was around one in the afternoon. When me and Misa woke up, she fed me and the baby, then got back on this dick. That was around eight, and now I was squinting while looking at my phone. The time was two in the morning. When I saw Kenni's number, I picked up the phone.

"Ken, you good?"

She sniffled into the phone. "I saw my mother."

"Damn, babe. You good?" I didn't give a damn about Terri but seeing how the shit bothered my baby made me upset.

"She looks so bad. Super skinny and her face is so sunken in," she sobbed into the phone. "I spent all day up there with her."

"Did her personality change?"

"No."

"Then babe, why are you crying?"

"Because my mother is dying, Maurice. It doesn't matter how she acts, she's still my mother." She continued to cry into the phone. I was confused on why the fuck she was calling me at two in the morning.

"Ight. I'm sorry. How did the visit go?"

"She was in and out because of her pain medicine. We spoke a little. She told me about an envelope she gave you when you came to the house to get my stuff," I had forgot all about that shit. I think I had tossed it out or something.

"I don't remember."

"Well, she told me about my father. She was actually raped while on vacation and that's how she got me."

"Word. Damn."

"She told me that she had drunk too much and was trying

189

to get back to her room. My father was there with his friends on the beach and volunteered to walk her back to her bedroom," she sniffled. "He brought her to the beach and had his way with her. She said she never knew his name or anything. A couple weeks later, she found out that she was pregnant with me. That was what was in the envelope. A letter from her."

"So, she knows nothing about your father?"

"Other than him being Dominican, no," she sighed into the phone. "She hated me because I was a constant reminder of her being raped." She sobbed hard. I wished I was near to hold her. Hearing some shit like this from your dying mother couldn't have been easy.

"I'm so sorry, Ma. When you come home, we'll talk about this more. We can find him," I offered.

"Why? Why would I want to have a conversation with a man that raped my mother? He doesn't know how much he fucked up my childhood. My mother literally hated me because I reminded her of him. He ruined my life by putting a baby into her, which she hated. She hated me so much... you have no idea." She continued to cry.

"Ken, I need you to calm the hell down. Your mother had a lot of shit going on. It's not like she treated your brothers any better, and she actually consented to fucking their pops. Stop blaming yourself. Your mother's demons are her own and she'll have to answer to that shit soon."

"I guess. I'm going to shower and get some sleep." She sighed.

"Ight. Love you," I looked at the phone because she ended the call. For now, I was going to let that shit rock because she was upset.

Misa put her arms around me. "Everything alright, baby?"

"Yeah, her moms is dying and she going through a lot."

Misa kissed me on the lips and fumbled with my dick. "That's too bad... I feel for her."

"Babe, I'm not in the mood right now. Come lay on me," I told her. My dick wasn't in the mood to be fucked right now. Kenni was on my mind. Despite putting her through all that I have, I still hated to see her hurting. Her mother wasn't worth shit and still, she felt her mother's pain. I wanted to be near her so I could hug her and let her cry on me. Instead, I was miles away.

Misa had made breakfast before she took Kia to her moms and then went to take her test. I laid in the bed flipping through the channels and sending India and Mercedes money for my kids. When I called Kenni this morning she was still asleep and told me that she would call me back when she woke up. I closed my eyes for a quick minute, then popped my eyes up when I heard my phone ringing. India's name popped across the screen and I smirked. I knew money would make her ass want to call me. Instead of the usual amount, I sent her ass five dollars.

"You're a stupid bitch. It takes for me to send you five dollars to let me see my kids?" I answered the phone. She didn't even deserve a damn introduction like most.

"Bridge, get to the hospital now. I really fucked up. Oh god, I really fucked up," she said over and over again.

Leaning up, I pressed the phone to my ear hard. "India, what the fuck you talking about?"

"I didn't mean to. He's so fast now and curious that it happened so quick," she spoke in broken sentences.

"What the fuck are you talking about?"

"They're going to take my babies from me. I know they are. Bridge, get here please!" she screamed into the phone pleading.

"Send me a text with the hospital. I'm on my way." My heart was beating out of my chest as I quickly got dressed. She sent the address and I locked up Misa's crib and headed to the hospital.

I arrived in fifteen minutes and quickly made my way to the pediatric wing. After getting the visitor pass, I walked through the double door and to the nurse's section in that wing. She showed me to the room where India was a fucking mess. It had been over a month and change since I saw her or the kids. She was skinny as fuck and her hair was unmanaged. She had on a pair of sweats that were three sizes too big for her. The only thing that fit her good was a tank top she wore under the cardigan that could wrap around her body four times. When she saw me, she rushed over to me and hugged me.

"What the fuck happened?" I shoved her off me and went over to my son laying in the hospital bed. He was asleep. I reached down and kissed him on the forehead. My son was my world and I knew I didn't make as much time as I should for my kids, still I loved them.

"He was supposed to be watching TV. I had my drink on the floor while getting Mya a new diaper, and he drunk the whole cup. He was drunk and I thought it would leave his system, but then he wouldn't wake up after I put him down."

I put my hand back and slapped the shit out of her. "I told you about drinking in front of my fucking kids, India. What you do is your business, but the moment one of my kids are hurt, that's a fucking problem!" I yelled so loud that spit flew from my mouth.

"Excuse me." A lady with a wrinkled suit jacket and papers in her hand entered the room. "I'm Regan McKee. I'm the case worker that is assigned to your case. The doctor has informed me of everything going on with your son." She reached her hand out and shook me and India's hand.

"Are you kidding me? I've been here since last night and not once has the doctor came in and informed me of anything!" India yelled. She looked like she hadn't slept in a fucking week.

"At this time we're removing the children from the home." My damn heart dropped because that meant my kids were going into foster care if they didn't allow me to take them.

"Oh my god. Not my babies... please. It was an accident. I love my babies!" India screamed out and fell to the floor.

"What exactly is going on with my son?"

"Your son had drank so much alcohol that he had low blood sugar, which resulted in him having a seizure in his sleep. The doctors are testing his brain to see if he has any brain damage. The doctors were able to get him stable and awake, but he suffered another seizure, so he's in an induced coma for now," she explained and I had to sit down. That shit brought tears to my fucking eyes and hate to my heart for India.

"W...what about me? Will I be able to get my kids?"

"You're the biological father?"

"Yeah."

"Do you live in the home with her?"

"No, me and my girlfriend live together. We can do a home visit and shit right now. Don't put my kids in foster care... they have a home with me," I pleaded with this lady. I had never pleaded for anything in my entire life, but for my kids I would.

She looked over the papers. "I see there is two kids in the home."

"Yes. My son and daughter."

"Where's the daughter?"

"S...she's with my neighbor," India sniffled with tears and

snot all over her face. The bitch had a drinking problem and she popped Ecstasy occasionally. I didn't think she had a problem, but seeing her right now told me that she had a big problem.

"We'll need to get your daughter and hold her tonight. I can put you on my schedule for the first home visit of the day."

"Please, please. Thank you, Ma'am. I really appreciate that."

"I'll send the doctor in to speak with *you*." She cut her eyes at India, who was still on the floor.

Soon as she left, my hands balled and I wanted to beat the shit out of her. I knew I couldn't because I needed my kids to be able to be granted permission to come with me.

"You're done, bitch. You're never going to see those kids ever again," I snarled and looked at her.

"I made a mistake, Bridge. I love my kids. You're never fucking there and then you want to show up like dad of the fucking year!" she screamed, with spitting landing on the floor in front of my sneaker. "It's me having to deal with them all day with no fucking help."

"Your stupid ass shouldn't have tried to trap me. You wanted these kids and now you got them and realize that shit too much for you? I don't fucking feel bad for your stupid ass. Mercedes is about to have another one of my babies, and I bet she don't get strung off Ecstasy and fucking alcohol."

"You're fucking toxic. The way you beat on Kenni and make her feel like a piece of shit. You think I want my daughter and son being raised by you? You're a fucking monster."

"Yet, soon as I want to give you this toxic dick you jumping on it like a fucking addict. You don't have no choice on how me and my girl raise these kids," I walked out the room to find the doctor.

Kenni loved my kids and I knew she would raise them with me. I didn't even have time to call her, I knew that she wouldn't have a problem. We didn't have no baby right now and we had nothing but space for the kids. Kenni has been wanting a baby, and when she lost our babies she became depressed whenever babies were mentioned. I knew this was like handing her a gift wrapped. Two babies for the price of one. I knew for sure; India wasn't getting my kids back. She had two other kids that she had failed and my dumb ass trusted her to raise my damn kids. That was something that would never happen again.

Thirteen

Kenni

I POPPED one of my birth control pills and then showered for the day. It had been two weeks since I had been back from New York. Spending time with my mother was hard. She was still bitter, hateful and angry at the world. Except, this time she wasn't angry because she had kids and lost her beauty. She was angry because she was dying. Like, it was anybody else's fault but her own. I could have saw her once and never saw her again, but something in my spirit wouldn't allow me to just go once. I spent the few days that I was in New York with her. Haze was right there waiting for me when I got back to Saylor's house. We spent those few days together, which was needed. He made me so happy and showed me how a woman was supposed to be treated. I had never had an example of how a man should treat a woman. Haze showed me and made sure I knew how beautiful and cherished that I was. It was a welcomed change from the way Bridge treated me.

When I got out the shower, I quickly hid my birth control pills in the plant in the bathroom. Bridge thought I was going to get knocked again, and I refused. I didn't want a baby with him. The way he knocked me around and caused me to lose our others, I'd rather not relive what happened again. So, as much as he tracked my period, I knew his ass thought he was going to get me pregnant. While he ran around doing his dirt, I went and got on birth control. It had been a year since I was on birth control and his ass knew nothing about it. I went to the next town to go to the doctor and then to the pharmacy near my doctor's office. We didn't need a baby, especially with Mya and Maurice Jr. living with us. It was a surprise when I came home and Mya's crib was in our bedroom. I wasn't surprised that India got the kids taken away. Hell, I thought she would have gotten them taken sooner. Maurice Jr. was thankfully alright. He had to take medication for his seizures and had appointments each week to meet with his specialist to make sure no brain damage occurred when he had the seizure in his sleep. Guess who took him? Me.

Since the kids had moved in, it had been me who had been taking care of the kids. Bridge continued to live life however he wanted while I was being their mother. He didn't want India to have anything to do with the kids, and I should have respected his wishes. I allowed her to come to the house and see the kids during nap time. Maurice Jr. talked too much now and he would have ratted me out to his father. Like today, Bridge said he had to drive to Philly with Brix for business. I called India and told her she could come over. I should have wanted to beat the shit out of India and never speak to her again, but some part of me felt sorry for her. She had to raise those kids alone. Bridge was nowhere to help, except with some money here and there. Money didn't solve issues. Mothers went through some real shit, and even if she trapped Bridge, he still should have been there as a father. I wasn't worried about the shit she did to me, because she was paying with her karma now.

"I know it's only been a few weeks, but they're getting so big." While she sat in the kid's playroom, I took a quick shower so I could take Maurice to his appointment. Juggling one kid was hard, but two was damn near impossible.

"Kids grow quick," I kept it short. "Want something to drink?"

"Sure." She sat down at the counter. I grabbed us two bottles of water and handed her one. "Kenni, I really want to apologize for fucking Bridge behind your back. We were friends and I betrayed you."

"If you could do something like that to me, we were never friends. I'm good. You don't need to apologize. The only reason I'm doing this is because I know hard it is to be a single mother."

"I appreciate it. The case worker has me enrolled in AA. I have to go twice a week, find a job within the next two weeks, and I'm about to be evicted because Bridge won't send me money."

"Why should he? The kids are here with him," I didn't agree with a lot of shit that Bridge did, but the money situation I agreed on. Why should she be paid like she has the kids?

"I guess I deserve that."

"I'm not here to judge you because that's not my job. I know the kids miss you and you miss them. This situation isn't ideal. I didn't sign up to be a step-mother at all. However, I love those kids and want to make sure they're taken care of."

"I thank you for that."

"No need. I'm not doing it for you or Maurice," I went and started getting Maurice Jr's snacks ready for when he woke up.

"I debated if I should tell you this or not, but I appreciate everything you're doing for the kids, and even letting me see them during nap time once a week. I can't keep this from you and you deserve to know."

"What?" I was counting out crackers for Maurice and grabbing his juice.

"Mercedes is having another baby. Bridge is the father," she revealed and I dropped the apple juice box. "He told me the night that we were at the hospital. I don't think he meant to tell me, but he was so mad and yelling so it kind of slipped out."

"Thank you for telling me."

"You're not mad?"

"You have two of his kids. Why shouldn't she have another kid?" I replied. As angry as I was, I wasn't about to show India how hurt and angry that I was.

"I'm sorry I told you. Bridge doesn't deserve you and has never deserved you."

"So, why did you take the first chance to fuck him?"

"Because I wanted what you had. Kenni, you've always had niggas running around and wanting you. Me, I couldn't get a nigga without sucking his dick. Niggas loved you and flocked to you like a bee does honey."

"You see all of this," I waved my hand around the state of the art chef kitchen. "This means nothing to me. The cars, clothes, and all of it doesn't mean shit to me. You can have this shit," I slightly vented. "You wanted what I had without fully knowing what came with it."

"You're right. I don't know how many times Bridge has raped me or done some evil shit and I've kept my mouth shut."

I could relate. When Bridge wanted something, he didn't give a damn how he was going to get it. Long as he got it. There was a few times that he forced himself inside of me. He felt because I was his girlfriend that it wasn't rape. It was rape, didn't matter if I was his girlfriend or not.

"You have a chance away from him. Get your shit together and get your babies back and move the fuck away from him," I warned her. "India, do you really want him raising your kids?"

"You're right." She looked at her phone. "I have to get to this meeting. Thank you again," she said, as I walked her to the door.

I grabbed my phone and dialed Haze's number. "What's good, Beautiful?" I loved the way he answered the phone when I called him.

"Nothing. Making the kid's snacks before this doctor appointment. What are you doing?" I smiled and continued putting together their snacks.

"About to take Whitney and Brittany to the mall. She wanted to spend time together," I couldn't help but to feel jealous. She had Haze and I wanted him so bad.

"Have fun," I dryly replied.

"You really going to act like that?"

"Sorry."

"You know I wanna be with you. I'm trying to keep the tension in the house down. We been arguing and shit."

"I know. I'm sorry for even acting that way."

"That's my girl. I can't front, I miss you."

"I miss you too... Are we still down for Miami at the end of the month?"

He chuckled into the phone. "You already know. I been counting down that shit since we made the plans." Haze wanted to spend time with me out of our states. The time in New York wasn't enough, so we decided to go to Miami.

I had already told Bridge that I was going to Miami to get my breast done. He believed me because I had been complaining about how small my breast were for years. I told him my consultation was at the end of the month and that Saylor was coming with me. He had been in his own head lately, so he told me that I better had lined up somebody to handle the kids because he didn't have time to sit in the house and watch kids all day. Jessica told me she would watch the kids for me. I couldn't wait to be around Haze on the beach and spending time together. I knew that Bridge had took Mercedes to Miami because his slipper was in one of her pictures on the beach. She was real careful not to post any pictures of him, but I recognized his slipper in the picture. I didn't bring anything up to him because I was saving it for the perfect time. He thought he was so slick, so while he was fucking in Miami and I was here playing a fool, I was about to fuck the shit out of Haze right in our suite and not feel guilty about it at all.

"I've been thinking about it too. I know it has only been two weeks, but I need a getaway, I'm so tired."

"He still got you taking care of the kids alone?"

"Yep. When he comes home he plays with them and expects me to put them to bed while he goes and unwind in the den. I'm so tired."

"That's fucked. You know what you have to do, and I know it's hard." He brought this up each time I complained about Bridge. He told me that I needed to leave, and I knew I had to leave. I was terrified to leave Bridge. He wouldn't leave me alone. I would always have to look over my shoulder because he wouldn't let me live in peace. He had told me plenty of times that he'd catch a case behind me leaving him.

"It's much easier said than done. It's so much that I have to do to leave him. Then where does that leave me? I've saved some money over the years, but not enough to live without him."

Bridge would hand me money like it was going out of style. I would take some and put the rest in a bank account that he didn't know about. I had some money to leave, but I was thinking about the future. What happened when I ran out of that money? How was I going to pay for shit?"

"You get a job, Kenni. You were the smartest chick in our school. You finished school early that's how smart you were. You telling me that you can't find a career?"

"How? Bridge made me drop out of college."

"Go back to college. I'll pay for everything until you graduate. I'll do what I need to make sure you're not getting your ass kicked every night."

I leaned on the fridge. "I can't ask you or Saylor to do that for me. It's something I'm going to have to figure out on my own."

"Kenni, I fucking love you. You know I've always loved you, but I love you and being around you makes me fall more and more in love with you. Still, I'm not going to sit here and wait for him to kill you. I'll distance myself from you before I let that happen."

His words were harsh, but true. I knew I couldn't expect him to play second while I tried to survive living with Bridge. "What about you? You're with Whitney."

"Like I keep telling you, I'll end all of this for you. Walk away from it all now because I love you that much."

"You love me more than Whitney? You've been with her before me."

"Yeah, I've always loved you. Getting to know the real you caused me to fall even more in love with you."

"That's sweet."

"I'm pulling up to the mall. We'll talk later."

"Okay," I said before we ended the call. When I heard Mya cry, I knew it was time to get them ready and head to Maurice Jr's doctor appointment.

After the doctor's appointment, I took Maurice Jr. to the park to run around while I watched holding Mya. He had fun and met some other little boys around his age. His mother handed me her card and told me she has playdates all the time. I know I wanted a baby and had said it in the past but being handed that flyer made me not want kids. This wasn't the life that I wanted. Having kids with Bridge felt so wrong and dirty. I hated it because I wanted to be a mother, but then when I thought about my life and situation, it made me not want to be a mother. It scared the shit out of me to have a kid with a man that I was supposed to love. Having Maurice Jr. and Mya move in with us showed me the kind of parent he was going to be. It was one that I wasn't interested in being with. The thought of Mercedes having another baby by him made me want to puke. Did she not want better for her and her children? I guess she did get better. After all, she did get a trip to Miami with him and their daughter.

When I pulled into the driveway, both Mya and Maurice Jr. were fast asleep in their car seats. I killed the engine and did the daunting task of getting both kids out of the car at the same time. I grabbed Mya's car seat first, then gently tapped Maurice

Jr. He stirred in his sleep, then woke up. I thanked the gods that I didn't have to carry him into the house again.

"You had a good sleep?" I unstrapped his buckle and helped him out the car. He nodded his head and ran up the steps to the door.

After letting us into the house, I unstrapped Mya and put her in the highchair. "Eat, eat." Maurice pointed to his mouth.

"Okay, let's wash our hands like a big boy... okay?"

He nodded his head and we headed to the bathroom. That's when I realized that Bridge was home. He was fast asleep in his den with the TV on mute. After we washed Maurice's hand, I sent him in there to wake his father.

"Aw man, you got me," I heard him tickling Maurice. While he played with him, I wiped Mya's hands down and got dinner together. The kids didn't give a damn what I made as long as they had food. I made a quick hamburger helper meal, and some sweet potatoes and ground chicken for Mya.

"The phone," I heard Bridge call when the house phone started to ring. He had one right in there with him and couldn't take two minutes to answer the phone.

Grabbing the phone off the foyer table, I walked back into the kitchen. "Hey Ju," I smiled. It had been a little while since we spoke or hung out. I knew she was going through a lot and wanted to give her space.

"Well, hello stranger." She laughed.

"I know, I know... I miss you though."

"I miss you too. It's so much that we haven't talked about... like me being pregnant," I nearly dropped the phone.

"Pregnant? Serious?"

"Yes. I found out a little while ago and wanted to keep it hush from the family."

"Oh wow. I'm so happy. This is what you guys have been wanting. How's Brix feeling?"

"Girl, praying for a little girl. I'm praying too. We're so happy and blessed."

"I'm glad."

The line grew quiet.

"You know your little friend was trying to get Brix to cheat on me, right?" whenever she mentioned *my* little friend, I knew she was talking about Saylor.

"Stop playing."

"He told me everything," I could tell she was lying by the tone of her voice. You know you spend so much time around a person you start being able to tell when they're lying, uncomfortable, or angry without them having to tell you? Juleena was one of those people. I knew when she was lying, angry or just uncomfortable about a situation. There was more to the story and she wasn't trying to tell it.

"I had no clue, Juleena."

"Girl, I know... they kept it between them good. We're back good and focusing on our family. I hope *she* is finding her some business, other than my man's business."

"Like I told her, I don't discuss y'all business to the other person. If you wanna know, call her up. Brix probably has the number," I moved the phone away and laughed.

"You think that's funny, hoe," she gave me a fake laugh. "Anyway, I want to link up to get our nails or something done. I know you have the kids, so I'll ask mama to come over to your house."

"Just come over, or I'll come over there. I already asked her to watch them when I go to Miami."

"Miami? For what?"

"I'm getting my breast done and have an appointment down there."

"After this baby I'm going to need to get some work done, so make sure you give me the number."

"You know I got you." The other line beeped. "Ju, let me call you back. It's my other line."

"Okay, girl."

I clicked over on the other line. "Hello?"

"Hi, this is Dr. Clemmings from Methodist hospital," I already knew it was my mother's doctor. I had put my number in her file so they could keep me updated.

"Hi, Dr. Clemmings. This is Kenni."

"Hey Kenni. I hate to call you with this news." He paused. "Your mother passed an hour ago in her sleep. I had a few patients so I wasn't able to call. However, I wanted to be the one who called you and delivered the news."

"Nooooo!" I screamed out and scared Mya. I dropped the spoon I was holding and cried out.

Bridge came rushing into the kitchen and caught me before I fell from my feet. "What happened, baby?" he asked, concerned while grabbing the phone. Everything was a blur. I shouldn't have cared so much, yet I did. My mother wasn't shit, and even after visiting her she still hadn't changed. Still, I cared and it was a pain in my heart. Bridge finished the conversation and then pulled me into his arms. "I'm sorry, ma. I really am. I love the shit out of you."

I shook away from him and sobbed harder. "You don't fucking love me!" I screamed and backed away from him. "You've never fucking loved me!"

"Ma, what the hell are you talking about?" I could tell he was confused. Hell, I was confused too. All of my anger and sorrow was coming up and coming up in pieces. I was sad about my mother, yet the anger of him getting Mercedes pregnant again came up.

"You fucking Mercedes in Miami and getting her pregnant again! You didn't think I would find out! Lord knows what you were doing when I visited my mother a few weeks ago!" I continued to scream.

"It was an accident, Ken. We were drunk and shit happened. She was there with her moms and we ran into each other," he lied. Bridge bit his lip when he was lying.

"Oh spare me the fucking lies. I'm in this house taking care of *your* kids while you out here fucking other bitches. You think that's fair to me? I'm the one holding down this house and life and you can't even keep your dick to yourself!" I broke down and continued to sob. It all hurt so much.

"You really that mad that I took a vacation with my daughter? Am I not supposed to make memories with my kids? We slept in separate rooms and got drunk at the bar. It just happened. If you're trying to make me pick between you and my kids, you fucking crazy."

I laughed. With a face full of tears I had the nerve to laugh. "Even you don't believe that shit that comes out of your mouth. Why would I make you choose between your kids? You've never put me first in anything, so I'm not surprised now," I chuckled and walked up to the bedroom. I heard him down there putting the kids in the playroom. He quietly entered the room while I laid on my side with my back to the door. He sat down and rubbed my head.

"I'm sorry. I keep fucking up and don't fucking deserve you. That was before I made my promise to God to change. Babe, I could have knocked your head off for the way you screamed at me, but I didn't."

Bridge would have slammed me against the wall for the way

that I screamed at him. Instead, he stood there and took me screaming at him. "Why do you keep doing this to me?"

"Babe, I'm fucked up. You know that... I wasn't raised right and my mama fucked me over... I'm trying to be a better man for you and for the kids. Be patient with me," he kissed me on the forehead.

Maybe he was trying to change? Could he change? It had been a while since he spoked to me soft and allowed me to get my anger out without busting me in the head.

"I'm trying, Maurice. You keep having me out here looking stupid... another baby. I can't do it," I sobbed.

"We don't even know if it's my baby. I strapped up with her," he said like it made it better. "I'm gonna finish dinner and put the kids to sleep. When I'm done, I'm gonna come hold you and order your favorite from the Chinese spot... okay?"

"Okay," I cuddled deeper into my pillow.

"See, your mom is gone... You don't have nobody that's going to look out for you, but me. I've been here since 08...I love you, Kenni."

I believed him. He had been there for me. Everyone else popped in and out. Bridge had been the one who took me out the hood and brought me into a mansion. He provided everything for me all he expected was a clean home and meal. I never had to work a job a day in my life.

"I love you too," I closed my eyes and allowed my sleep to take over. My heart and head hurt. My mother was dead.

Haze

I LAUGHED when Kook told me that Whitney was back fucking with Rod. I knew she had to be because of the way she had been asking. We hadn't fucked in weeks, and she hadn't been on me about spending Saturdays with her and Brittany. The only reason we had went out last week was because I mentioned it. Whenever Kook came with some information, he always had facts to back that shit up. Meeka had saw her hugged up with Rod at some backyard party. She knew I wouldn't have found out because I don't do the party scene unless it's at my lounge. Niggas were to jealous hearted and no nigga wasn't about to catch me lacking. She said they were kissing and acting like nobody else was at the party. All those Philly trips were bullshit. She was probably right here in Virginia with Rod's ass. Whitney always acted like she was obsessed with whatever the fuck Rod was doing. I don't think she ever got over him fucking her cousin.

"Nigga, he fucking your bitch and you acting like the shit funny. Wanna roll up on that nigga?"

"Nah."

"You being pussy."

"It don't have shit to do with me being pussy. I'm not about to risk going to jail for pussy that was never mine. If I gotta shoot a nigga over pussy, it was never mine in the first place."

Kook screwed his face up. "Nigga, please. I'd air the entire block out behind Meeka." He slapped his chest a few times.

"We're two different people," I shrugged. I wish I could say I was hurt or even angry behind the shit with Whitney. I wasn't mad because I knew that she had never got over her ex. A few things had showed me that she wasn't over him and I chose to ignore that shit. All I wanted was for her to get her shit out my crib and let him put her up in a new house.

"Clearly. What you gonna do?"

"Nothing."

"You gonna continue to let her live there?"

"Oh nah, she gotta bounce.... I'm not arguing or fighting for something that I don't want anymore. I did my shit too."

"You and Kenni never fucked."

"What we did was worse.... She got my heart."

"Oh you fake deep ass nigga," Kook laughed.

Hans was in New York. He had come up last weekend to make sure shit was good and to catch up with me and Kook. That nigga took Saylor to Thailand and had fell even more in love with her. He was talking about moving to New York and trying to set shit up there. If he felt like it was a good move, I was going to follow his lead. He was my brother and had never showed me wrong, so I was riding with him.

"Be quiet, nigga," I laughed.

I called Kenni from my phone and she denied my call again. All week I hadn't heard from her. We were supposed to meet this weekend to head to Miami and she hadn't said shit to me.

Not now.

Then when?

I'm not going to Miami. She text me back and I called her phone again. This time she answered. I could hear a baby in the background and kids playing.

"Yo, what the fuck is up?" Now, I was irritated because I had paid for everything so we could spend some time in Miami together. Lowkey, that had been the one thing holding me together. The thought of laying on the beach with her and sipping cocktails. Nights filled with expensive dinners and sex on the balcony of the suite I booked for the both of us.

"Haze, right now isn't a good time." She whispered into the phone.

"Then when? I been hitting you all week and haven't heard from you once," I barked into the phone. I hated to raise my voice at her. She knew how important this trip was and for her to cancel the week of is what pissed me off.

"Can you watch her, please? Thanks," I heard her say. "I'm at a playdate right now and can't talk about this."

"Why the fuck you been ignoring my calls, Kenni?"

She sighed into the phone. "I can't do this anymore. Me and Bridge have been working on things and stuff is good."

"For right now. What happens when you bust him in the head? Huh? What happens when that nigga fucking goes upside your head?"

"He has," she admitted. I could hear her voice crack when she spoke about it. That nigga could never keep his hands to himself. "I was in the hospital for two days because of it. Haze, I don't want to hold your life up anymore. I want you to be happy," she cried into the phone and it made me angry. It made me want to fucking yell, scream, and go rescue her.

"You need to leave. I'm coming to get you, Ken. He's going to kill you."

"No. I know how to deal with him. Please, leave me alone... Go make Whitney happy. She deserves you, not me."

I put the phone against my chest and held in the tears that wanted to fall out of my eyes. "Ken—" she ended the call.

Kook looked at me and shook his head. "You good, man?"

"Nah," I sighed.

He touched my shoulder. "Hopefully she'll find the strength to leave. You can't make her leave, man."

He was right. As much as I wanted Kenni to leave, I couldn't force her to leave. It was something that she had to do.

She had to gather that courage to want better and leave Bridge. He had a mental hold on her that was so fucking tight. She thought she deserved the life she lived. She thought him putting his hands on her was love. Although she would tell me she knew he didn't love her, I think she said that for me. I believed that she thought Bridge loved her and that him putting his hands on her was him showing her love. I sat with Kook for a little while before I headed home. When I came through the door, Whitney was cooking dinner. Me and Kook had tossed back a few beers before I bounced and I was feeling those shits.

"Hey Haze... I made tacos tonight. Brittany is staying at her dad's tonight," she informed me. Good. Easier to kick her ass out tonight. "You good, babe?"

"Yeah. I'm straight," I grabbed two more beers from the fridge and sat at the kitchen table. Whitney put the tacos in front of me. Thinking about Kenni had me not wanting to eat. I thought about her the entire ride home, and I lived thirty minutes from Kook's house.

"You sure? You look like your gold fish died or something." She sat down and put some sour cream on her taco before she took a bite.

"Yeah," I finished the beer and watched as she ate her taco like she hadn't been cheating on me. This was what made me hate females like her. She had a good ass man and she wasn't satisfied. She wasn't happy because she wanted the nigga that fucked her cousin and got her pregnant. Even with me having my little shit with Kenni, it didn't compare to her fucking that nigga and then coming to lay her head under my roof. I provided for both Whit and her kid. I never complained or acted like it bothered me because it didn't. In fact, I loved doing for her daughter because I treated her like she was mine.

We had little dates with just us, and she loved me like I loved her.

"So, I've been thinking about getting Brittany a dog for her birthday," she spoke up, and I laughed. "What's funny?"

"Nothing."

She dropped her taco and looked at me. "On the real, what the hell is going on with you? You've been acting real funny since you walked through the door."

"Shit, you would act funny if you found out your bitch was fucking her baby daddy behind your back." Her silence spoke volumes. She didn't even need to defend herself because the look on her face and her loss of words was enough for me to know that it was true.

"Look, it just happened. I was at a backyard party and he showed up. He was pissed about my cousin and we were drinking... I didn't mean for it to happen like that," she admitted.

"It just happened at the party?"

"Yes. I swear. Each time I pick up Brittany, he tries to make it more. I realized that I made a mistake and wanted to move past it. Baby, I'm so sorry. I should have told you."

"You didn't fuck him?"

Silence again.

"Yes, but that night. He drove me to his house and we had sex. My cousin was over my grandmother's house for her nephew's party. After we had sex I regretted it," she started to cry. "I don't want to lose you. I love you and what we have."

"You can't lose something you already lost," I told her. "I want you out the crib by the end of the month. Ask that nigga to find you a place or go to your mama's crib," I got up from the table.

"Haze, you've been distant lately. His attention felt good. I don't know where your mind is half the time. When you come in, you go shower and go right to bed. We haven't had sex. Don't blame all of this on me."

"There was someone. I didn't stick my dick inside of her."

She stood up and wiped her hands on her jeans. "We both messed up. I love you so much, Haze. I want to fix this."

I sighed. I couldn't front like I didn't love the shit out of Whitney. We had both been in a different place these past few months. I had been consumed with Kenni, and I had been blowing her off. It wasn't an excuse for what she did, but I had to admit when I was wrong. Once me and Kenni connected, it was like I tossed Whitney to the back burner.

"I know," I sighed. "I fucked up."

She had tears coming down her face as she walked toward me. "I love you, baby. I really do. I fucked up and I'm sorry... I really am," I pulled her into my arms and we stood in the kitchen hugging.

"Yeah, I fucked up too," I admitted. "I love you, Whit." As much as it hurt to leave Kenni alone, she had to want to leave. I couldn't fuck up my life because she wanted to play games. I don't think she ever wanted to leave. I think she loved having someone to vent to, and someone who understood her and made her feel beautiful again. She fell in love with feeling how she used to feel when we were younger. I knew one thing; I couldn't continue to allow her to put me on this Ferris wheel. If it was meant for me and Kenni to be, we would ... be.

Fourteen

Bridge

"I'M SO sick of this shit, Maurice. Where else would I get an STD from?" Kenni yelled. She was getting on my nerves with this yelling shit. I had been trying real hard not to hit her ass, then she brought this shit up. She didn't learn from a month ago when she had to sit in the hospital for two days.

I had a lot of shit going on right now and Kenni was adding onto that shit. My connect was talking about pulling out from me. He was talking about how the sales were making sense. I was late paying him last month and now the nigga was worried that I wasn't making money no more. He mentioned some nigga in New York that was about to make him a lot of money from New York to Virginia and everything in-between. When I asked who it was, he told me he couldn't tell his business to me. Money was getting low and niggas were getting robbed. Brix told me that he was out the game so I was trying

217

to find someone to replace him. I had a lot of shit coming down on me and she wanted to yell about a fucking STD.

"The kids are sleep. You need to chill the fuck out... who the fuck you been fucking?"

If looks could kill she would have killed me with one eye. "Me? What the fuck are you talking about? I don't fuck anyone except you. Who the fuck are you fucking?" I knew that bitch from the club last week would get me in trouble. I didn't have time for a condom and slipped in while in the VIP section. She fucked me right there on the couch and had me take her number.

"What your doctor give you? Cause if you got something then I got something," I asked and she rolled her eyes.

"I'm so stupid. I swear I'm so stupid," tears fell down her cheek. "After Mercedes I should have been done, but my stupid ass sat here and continued to be with you." She vented to herself.

"Kenni shut the fuck up. I haven't fucked no other bitch," I continued to lie and she continued to vent to herself. "Your ass better chill out before you wake my damn kids."

"I could have been so happy with him. I fucking gave up a life of happiness to be pissing and it burning."

"Who the fuck you could have had a happy life with." She realized she fucked up and remained silent. "I'm not going to repeat this shit."

"Nobody," she said.

"Kenni I heard what I heard," I got up and she backed up away from me.

"You get mad about any nigga I mention but treat me like shit. Any of your niggas would be happy or make me happy."

See, I ignored the credit card statements when they said Virginia on them during the time I was in Miami. I figured it was an old charge that was just now popping up. The accountant didn't have no problem with it, so I didn't see the need to question Kenni about it. Now, it was all making sense to me. She was fucking around with some other nigga. That was the reason she had been walking around all happy before. Now, she seemed like she lost her best friend or some shit. But, before. She was a different person. Not talking back or none of that shit.

"Who the fuck you was fucking you dirty bitch?" I had been so consumed with my baby mamas and kids that I wasn't paying her no damn mind.

She took off out the bedroom door and I followed right behind her. "Nobody, baby. I didn't have sex with nobody."

I grabbed hold of her arm before she made it down the rest of the stairs. "Stop fucking lying to me. The credit card statement to Virginia, then you leaving me to stay out there for two weeks. I'm not fucking stupid," I held her arm so hard that she screamed for me to let go.

"Please, you're hurting me," she pleaded with me.

I let her go and pushed her down the rest of the stairs. "Tell me what the fuck his name is, Kenni and stop playing with me.

"I'm over you hurting me. I'm leaving," she struggled to her feet and then headed to the kitchen. She was limping and crying out in pain.

"You ain't going no damn where. You think you gonna leave me? Huh? After all the shit I've done for you.... I took you out the hood with your jealous ass mama and roach infested apartment. I upgraded your life and taught you how to ride and suck dick," I pinned her up against the wall. Holding her around the neck, I looked her in the eyes. "I fucking love you and been showing you my love. And how do you repay me? You go out and fuck another nigga behind my back. I'm the one breaking my back so you could live like this. Do you ever ask me how the fuck I'm doing or if I'm good?" I continued to talk while squeezing her neck tighter and tighter. She clawed at my arms and I continued.

"B..ridge... please," she gasped.

My mind had went somewhere different. "I'm this close to losing all I've worked for and you want to question me about a bitch that I fucked. I got kids and a house to try and pay for and you always worried about you," I continued to choke her until I was satisfied. "Get the fuck up and clean yourself and this kitchen up. Don't even bring your ass back upstairs... sleep down here bitch," I headed upstairs and continued to watch the game, like I had been when she came up here screaming about an STD. She had the nerve to be worried about that shit when I had to find a new connect that had the same grade of coke we've been providing for years. I had a lot of fucking pressure on my back and she thought that this shit was most important. I dozed off sitting in the seating room of our bedroom thinking about all the shit I had to deal with soon as I woke up. I knew Kenni's ass better had the house spotless.

I rolled over and grabbed my phone. It had been ringing all morning and I had been silencing it because I wanted to sleep. Looking at the time, I had slept to twelve in the afternoon. Grabbing the phone, I put it to my ear.

"What's good?" I yawned into the phone.

"You forgot we have an appointment this morning?" She snapped on the other line. It had slipped my mind.

"Shit... let me get up. I'll meet you there."

"It's over, Bridge. I had to drive myself." She sighed.

"My bad. I had a crazy night and I'm just now waking up."

"Isn't it always something... bye." She ended the call.

Mercedes needed her ass knocked around too. God forbid I missed an appointment and she would have a heart attack.

I went to piss and take care of my morning hygiene before heading downstairs. I heard Mya screaming at the top of her lungs, so I went to her bedroom. She was standing on the side of her crib screaming. Her face was red, so I could tell she had been screaming for hours. I peeked into Maurice Jr's room and he was making a fucking mess in his room. He had shit smeared all over his walls and toys every damn where. The baby powder had been played all over. The room smelled like shit and baby powder.

"Kenni! Where the fuck are you?" I quickly headed down the stairs and looked in the guest rooms downstairs and the garage. Her car was still there, so her slick ass didn't try and leave. I walked into the kitchen and all the air had been knocked out of my lungs.

Epilogue

Six Months Later...

SAYLOR

DEAR KENNI,

LIFE ISN'T the same without you. I miss every day and want to call you. When you were alive, I never thought you would leave me. I always hated to talk on the phone, but I would get on the phone with you for years, if that meant that you would be brought back to me. I cry every night when you enter my dreams and tell me that I'm going to be alright. I want to grab you out of my dreams and tell you to come to me. You didn't deserve to be killed. Your life mattered. You were so young, so beautiful and so caring. You would give your all to help someone, and that's what I loved about you the most. You were always trying to see the good in someone, even when they didn't deserve that shit. You sacri-

ficed your life to be with a man that you knew was no good. Instead of seeing him for what he was, you continued to try and prove to me and everyone else that he was a good man, just misguided. I remember you told me that he wasn't loved enough as a child, and you planned to love him with everything you had. I laughed because it sounded foolish. You weren't loved enough as a child, I told you. You laughed and told me that Nana loved you enough and that was all that mattered.

It took a while for me to come to your grave site. Part of me didn't want to believe that you were gone. I wanted to believe that we were in the middle of a fight, and both of us were too stubborn to pick up the phone. I wanted to believe anything other than you were dead. We had plans. Big plans. We were supposed to visit Paris together and then go to Amsterdam and smoke so much weed that we would fly out the pub. We had plans. Baby, I want you to be here with me. The morning that I got the call that you were murdered was the best and worst day of my life. Best, because I had just taken a pregnancy test with Hans, and it was positive. I was excited to tell you that you were going to be an auntie. Worst, because I would never be able to physically tell you that you were going to be an auntie. Please hold onto my baby until she's ready to enter this earth. I know you're my angel, and I try to make peace with that, but it doesn't seem like it's enough.

Your death broke a lot of our hearts, especially Haze. He took your death even harder than I did. I think he blamed himself for not saving you. He wanted to love you and show you how a man was supposed to love a woman so bad, Ken. That man has always been in love with you. I don't think he ever stopped loving you. To this day, he speaks of you like you're still alive. I think like me, he refuses to believe that you're dead. Life goes on and Haze had to make peace with the fact that he'd never see your beautiful dimpled smile again. We would never hear your loud cackling laugh whenever you thought something was so funny. Haze and Whitney are still together. They are getting married next year and planning a huge wedding. I think Haze is kind of lost in the shuffle of your loss. He's numb to life right now and is going along with the punches. I check in with him often, and we lean on each other. Nobody will know just how hard your death impacted us.

Brix got out the game. He and Juleena broke up and he moved back to New York. He opened up a construction firm in the city, and he and Juleena are waiting on the birth of their son. He has a girlfriend that he's serious about. I met her a time or two. We have lunch every few weeks to touch bases. I think he's finally out of that stage of being obsessed with me. We both realized that too much had happened and we were better off as friends. Well, at least that's what I think. Juleena is still her dramatic self. She's prepping for the baby and running her salons. She's back on her feet. Jessica is helping her out and making sure that she's there to support her. Brix feels the need to update me on her life. I think he's just happy to be away and living his life on his own, without Juleena.

Me and Hans are good. He moved to New York and secured a connect here. We moved into a new house, bigger than my old one. Nana is no longer in the basement; she has a guest house in the back of the house. We're getting married next year. We want to settle into being new parents. He proposed to me two months ago when we were in Aruba. I love this man so much, and I'm glad you got to witness a small piece of it. He makes me feel whole and like a woman. I never have to question his motives. He'd die before he would hurt me and I loved him for it. I wish that I had been there to protect you better. I should have been there, even when you told me no. I wish every day that you got to experience a piece of the love I have. You deserve it, boo.

Sighs, Bridge is serving a life sentence. As much as Supreme was his mans, he loved the hell out of you. Coming into the house and seeing your dead body brought tears to his eyes. He turned Bridge in himself. He spent his money to give you a beautiful funeral. He was the one who called me and told me about you being killed. He blamed himself for not doing enough. I sat on the phone and heard a grown man cry like a baby. India was able to get her kids back. She got her shit together and got cleaned for her kids. She moved to California. She had some family out there and wanted something new. I never hear from her, because even in your death, that bitch fucked your man behind your back. We don't forgive – ever. Mercedes is working at a car wash because Bridge is broke. All of the cars, money and homes were gone. Turns out, he had a daughter by some chick name Misa. He was smart, he bought her townhouse out right in cash. Ken, they were engaged. She showed up to court rocking a ring on her finger and even took the stand and swore he was a good man. In the end, he was convicted and sentenced to life in prison.

Supreme and his wife welcomed a baby girl. They moved to Atlanta too. Supreme called to update me on his life and check on me. We kept in touch. Your birthday just passed and he flew into town so we could have a dinner for you. I miss you so much, Kenni. You have no idea how much I love and miss you. I pray every day that I will wake up from this bad nightmare. You meant the world to me. You were my first best friend, and sister. We grew up together and grew apart at some points of our lives, but the love always remained the same. Hold onto my baby until it's time to send her earth side. I love and miss you, sissy. I promise that when I touch down we'll talk over cloud cocktails. Continue being beautiful, beautiful.

Xoxo, Saylor.

I wiped the tears away from my cheeks and rubbed my

swollen stomach. Stepping forward, I put the letter on the tombstone, then kissed my finger and placed it on the picture of her tombstone. I sat the flowers I held in my other hand down and then walked back over to Hans. He held my hand and we stood there for a minute before walking away. I felt a brisk wind and smiled.

"She's here with us."

"We love you, Ken... keep looking out for us, sis."

"I love you, Kenni. Rest beautiful." Me and Hans held hands as we walked over to the car. A weight had been lifted off my chest. My best friend wasn't hurting anymore. She was free, and now she was my angel. I wished she was here, but God needed her more. He had other plans for her.

The End

Afterword

I wrote two endings to this book. The happy ending where she ended up with Haze, got married and had beautiful babies. Then, I wrote this ending. I debated if I wanted to give her a happy story. I sat on it for a while and decided to go with this ending. Mainly, because sometimes there aren't always happy endings. Sometimes, women in these type of relationships lose their lives. My heart goes out to every woman in this situation. Please find a way out before it's too late.

Thank you to all my readers that was on my ass to finish this series. This book was important. It was needed. If it saves one life, I've done my job. Thank you. – Jah.